LIGHT YEARS WISDOM

Noel Stevens

iUniverse, Inc.
New York   Bloomington

LIGHT YEARS WISDOM

Copyright © 2009 by Noel Stevens

iUniverse books may be ordered through booksellers or by contacting:

iUniverse
1663 Liberty Drive
Bloomington, IN 47403
www.iuniverse.com
1-800-Authors (1-800-288-4677)

Because of the dynamic nature of the Internet, any Web addresses or links contained in this book may have changed since publication and may no longer be valid. This is a work of fiction. All of the characters, names, incidents, organizations, and dialogue in this novel are either the products of the author's imagination or are used fictitiously.

ISBN: 978-1-4401-4308-3 (pbk)
ISBN: 978-1-4401-4309-0 (ebk)

Printed in the United States of America
iUniverse rev. date: 6/9/09

Author's Note

The USA Supreme Court forbad teaching creationism by God in US schools, opening the way for children to learn materialism only.

I wrote "text books" as fictional novels, as recommended reading for parents, for them to give their children at home. OUTSIDE THE CLASSROOM.

Microsoft's Bill Gates DISCOVERY INSTITUTE in Washington DC accepted these four books in early 2005. But on September 23rd, they rang to say they were returning them to me.

On September 26th 2005, DISCOVERY defended Dover

School, PA, at Harrisburg Courthouse – and DISCOVERY lost. My books would have saved them.

Eugenie Scott is Director of the National Centre for Science Education, and "Darwin's Watchdog". Darwin is rubbish; but she brought DISCOVERY to a crushing defeat in the Harrisburg Courtroom.

I have no computer: a friend tells me that the internet reports it cost DISCOVERY *one million dollars*. I don't know…

The judge wrote of "the breathtaking inanity" of the arguments by the Intelligent Designers. I understand they went back to Genesis!

In Light Years Wisdom, I have given hard science to strike down Darwin, and argue for Intelligent Design, for The Spirit.

Dover School had ordered a statement scorning evolution to be read to 9th grade biology students – IN THE SCHOOLROOMS. The statement said that Intelligent Design was an acceptable – if not better – alternative.

LIGHT YEARS WISDOM; IN THE NEVER-NEVER – CONVERSE WITH AN ARCHANGEL; THE FURTHEST HILLS OF ELSEWHERE and TIN GODS are four books which set out the knowledge that US pupils and students are not allowed to listen to. Dover School! You can recommend this book to the parents of your students! But this time around – nothing in writing!

All my thanks to Carolyn Neal for putting this book together with such affectionate care.

LIGHT YEARS WISDOM

"Light Years Wisdom is full of fascinating information..."

Brendan Walsh, Editorial Director, DARTON, LONGMAN, +
TODD, Britain's biggest Roman Catholic publisher of erudite
studies.

Part One

There was no foreboding, no warning unease.

On their second morning, Anne Moore stood at the bedroom window of their cabin and looked at the huge Rocky Mountains valley below. She turned to her husband, Ben, who everyone called Bo.

"You dressed, lover?"

"One shoe to go," he grinned.

Out in the dining room, Nicole and Fred had their gear ready, and Anne hurried to their own stuff.

Bo asked Fred, "Wonder whether we can get breakfast somewhere?"

Nicole called, "I was up here about four years ago, and there's a place down the road. Not the way we came up - but on the way to the cave."

Yesterday, a mountain man, on hearing that they were paleontology students, had drawn them a map of a cave.

Nicole stood up, and settled her pack on her shoulders. Plump, with big hips, she looked bigger in the bulky clothing and pack. Her serious eyes looked at them from the beauty of a perfect classical face.

They struggled into the packs, and packed their bags with the waterproof clothing and high rubber boots; they had to walk a hundred yards to the big 4 x 4, where they dumped their gear in the back.

Bo watched his wife with a slight smile as she tossed the weight. Slim, blonde, athletic, she had small breasts and a small face, but a grin that entranced him. He put his arm around her shoulders, and squeezed; then went around to the driver's seat.

Anne Grove got in beside her husband, with no inkling…

Fred and Nicole Moore got in the back.

Bo followed Nicole's directions as he drove, and they pulled up in front of a mountainside diner.

Inside was warm and fuggy, all the tables taken except a big one with a man sitting there alone. He waved to them, and they sat down, thanking him.

"Nothing more than my Christian duty," he said. They put him at about sixty, and looked at him guardedly. "You people know Christ?"

Nicole looked at him serenely. She asked, "Do they come to take your order, or you gotta go to them?"

"You go to the counter," he said, and Nicole, plump as she was, leapt to her feet and headed to the counter with surprising speed.

Fred said carefully, "We're college[1] students getting started on paleontology."

"Married really young, I see. What the Good Book tells us to." But he was suspicious.

Anne laughed, her smile infectious in her small face, and held up her wedding band. "The younger the better!" she said.

Mollified, the man said something about Christ, but Bo cut him short.

Bo said, "I'm into paleontology - that's early man. Anne here, my wife, is going to do paleichthyology - that's fossil fishes. Fred is going into paleozoology."

The man said, "All that pailee-onty - do you know that God created us, or do you believe Darwin?"

"Evolution's quite clear, "said Fred mildly.

---

[1] Known as *universities* outside of the USA

Nicole came back with a big tray, and handed out their breakfasts. They all poured coffee, and drank some down.

The older man said, "Saw some documentaries on evolution - what you call it. Saw this flatfish with both eyes on the top-side of its head. Know what the scientist tells us — expects us to swallow? Why, that dumb fish lay down flat on its side, generation after generation, for a million years, till it got a-tired of not seeing out of the bottom eye, and getting sand in it. So it somehow moved that bottom eye up to topside. Over that million years, laying on its side, it didna go hungry, and it didna get eaten.

"Y'know what happened? God made it that way, all at once, so from the word go it was able to stay alive."

Nicole asked mildly, "Why on earth should God do something as crazy as that?"

"Cause He figured out this was another way a fish could stay alive, could hide, could get food right down in the sand." He snorted. "The critter's so ugly, God probably got a laugh too," He looked at them belligerently.

They were eating a bit too quickly.

"That guy Darwin said the changes would all be tiny. Ain't no tiny changes. Just great big jumps, too complicated to happen by themselves."

Anne said, with her beguiling smile, "It all used be one big continent, that broke up, and the bits in between got lost."

"Yeah," he said. "That was on another documentary. You

must reckon people are dumb. We got airy-planes. I've seen guys looking for fossils in Africa, in Europe, Asia, the Gobi Desert - here in the States, and all over South America. Whoya kiddin'? You ain't found nothing anywhere because nothing's there."

He finished his coffee, and got up. "God bless you. It's great to be young, so young as youse are. You ask Christ for help, and you'll be okay."

They watched him walk firmly to the door, looked at each other, and laughed.

Bo took a deep breath. "In this day and age! Ignorance!" He gave a theatrical groan, and grinned.

They had to stop one hundred and fifty yards on from the half-mile marker.

They put on their wet-suits, and rubber boots, and threw the empty carryalls into the 4 x 4.

No one had any premonition.

They climbed clumsily for two hundred feet, and found the cave entrance.

Once, it could have been far bigger, because rock falls

surrounded it. A trickle of a stream came out and vanished under fallen logs.

Putting on their head lamps, they filed inside. It widened to about two hundred yards, the roof rose so high their lamps showed it but dimly.

Ten minutes on, they saw a new rock fall on the left, leaving a hole in the wall. Fred, slim, slid through it easily, and after a minute said, "Hey, come and have a look at this."

Anne slid through quietly, and Nicole and Bo squeezed in.

Fred shone his light on the wall behind him. They saw an immense arch, that had been bricked over. Then he swung his light over the huge chamber in front of them. The walls were even and glassy.

Fred said, "What sort of miners were these? What did they want to hide, bricking that arch up? And how did they get that finish, on the walls?"

They swung their lights around in astonishment.

"Let's have a look," said Bo, stepping out.

The chamber didn't get smaller. They saw it wasn't a chamber, but a tunnel of about two hundred and fifty feet in diameter, with smooth, glistening, glassy walls.

"These walls have been finished with tremendous heat," said Anne, uneasily.

Nicole stopped. "Or maybe the whole thing was tunnelled by terrific heat", she said, on the edge of fright.

They stopped, and gathered about her.

They listened.

"Utter silence," offered Fred.

"Might-a been an awfully long time ago. Nobody here now," Bo said slowly.

They thought about it for two minutes.

Fred said, "We can go another couple of hundred yards."

They walked slowly, and came to a wide bend.

They listened.

"Go as far as the bend?" said Anne.

After a minute, Fred led them. The bend straightened out, and they stopped.

Then they saw five columns, which broke into a blue glow. The columns were about seven feet high, about one foot thick, and spaced at about thirty feet, in a straight line across the tunnel.

Bo walked up to the nearest one, slowly, holding his left hand in front of his face.

He turned around. "I can't feel anything."

He stepped to one side, and walked forward, so that he'd have a column on each side. He stopped and waved his arm between them, then stepped forward.

The walls lit up in a whitish glow, and from the depths of the tunnel ahead, four robots on wheels came swiftly towards them.

Two of the robots were carts, with seats.

The other two wheeled robots raised an arm to point at them, and then at the seats.

Fred said thoughtfully, "Suppose we just turn back the way we came?"

Anne said, "I don't think they'd like that."

Bo nodded. "They look pretty strong to me."

Nicole went and sat down. She said, "Probably got ray guns or something worse."

The four robots ran for half-a-mile into the mountain, but uphill. They did about forty miles an hour, so they stopped after about thirty or forty seconds.

One robot went to a metal wall, held out one arm, and doors slid open.

They got off the seats, and walked into what looked like a lift cage. The doors closed, and the lift rose swiftly. When the doors opened, they saw two more robots with arms, that led them to a ramp leading into a flying saucer about two hundred and fifty feet in diameter.

The robot led them to a chamber with eight seats on each side, each seat with a porthole. It motioned for them to sit, and when they did, padded arms clamped their torsos and legs.

The robot went to a control panel, and plugged in its arm.

They heard humming, that got stronger and stronger.

They felt themselves rise, and suddenly through the portholes saw a mountain top. They rose swiftly, and saw hundreds of miles of mountains.

Then they saw the sea, and the coastline of the United States.

The earth dwindled - they could see it blue and white, hanging in space.

The moon approached, and they saw another flying saucer that must have been a hundred miles in diameter.

They settled down towards it; a hatch opened, and they were inside a brightly-lit hangar, with scores of Saucers.

The robot led them out, and they thought the hanger was at least a mile long.

A cart came; they took their seats, and it rolled to the wall of the hanger, where a hatch opened, and the cart rolled up a sloping tunnel for some three miles.

Bo said in wonderment, "They've pumped this full of air for us. The amount of air! Or do they breathe it?"

Anne said, "Or have they adapted their bodies to breathe it? I ought to be scared, but I'm not."

Fred said, "With this level of technology! We're like Indians out of the Amazons to them."

Nicole said, sounding frightened, "Suppose they want to impregnate us to get some sort of alien hybrid monsters."

Bo said soberly, "I think we know much too much."

The cart stopped, part of the wall slid open, and they went into a room with soft pink lighting, that slowly whitened.

They sat on the four chairs, and stared around the walls.

A door in front of them slid open, and an alien came in. He was tall, thin, with an olive-green skin, and wore a silvery suit that came up to his neck - if he had a neck. It came up under his chin. He had a long oval face with a pointed chin, slanting black eyes, no nose, and a thin straight mouth without lips.

He carried a black box, which spoke: "Welcome on board." The two men nodded.

The box went on, "You are indeed an embarrassment. You have found our emergency lifeboat. We have companions in human form living among you, and they use that craft in the mountain to come back to this base."

The four humans stared at the alien.

Bo asked, in a hoarse voice, "This base looked about a hundred miles across."

The alien stared at them, and then the box said, "About that."

After a pause, the box said, "We can read your thoughts. An hour before you boarded the craft in the mountain, you were talking to a man with almost no education, on the origin of life on this world. You have begun advanced studies on this, and yet this man tried to tell you the truth, while you are ignorant and refused to listen. You plan to finish your studies, and to proclaim these lies for the rest of your lives."

Anne stuttered, "You mean, we're Darwinists and he wasn't?"

The box said, "He understood the truth and you didn't. I know you earth people are ignorant, but to think that life put itself together is the deepest superstition.

"Please answer me. Do you wish us to wipe all memory of what has happened, and return you to your mountain cabin? Any talk about the cave will give you a total mind block?

"Or do you wish us to take you to another planet, some ten million light-years from here, to meet some elders, who will teach you wisdom? These men are thousands of years old, and their 'bodies' are no longer of matter.

"They will teach you of God. Do you believe in God?"

The four shook their heads.

"Why?"

Fred said, "No one can see Him. He doesn't stop suffering or blood-letting."

The box said, "Are you ladies afraid of being impregnated?"'

Anne and Nicole froze.

The box said, "It happened to mankind on this planet a couple of hundred thousand years ago, and more recently. Do you read your Bible?"

They shook their heads.

"In Genesis, it says that 'there were gods on earth in those days, who saw the daughters of men were fair, and they coupled with them.' What they did was manipulate their seed so that it could penetrate a human woman's ovum."

They sat in silence. No one wanted to say whether to go back to the cabin or go to the planet.

Anne said finally, "Ten million light years! Nothing can exceed the speed of light."

The box said, "Nothing with mass."

Bo said, "You annul the Higgs particle? But then what force exceeds the speed of light to push you?"

The box said, "Particles whose slowest speed is that speed of light, and which can move hundreds of thousands times faster than light. Tachyons."

The alien stared at them unblinkingly.

Fred said carefully, "We're going to cross part of the galaxy. But if at that speed we hit something…?"

The alien's eyes rested on Fred. The box said, "At that speed we're something like a haze — when we go through matter, it doesn't register. Also, at that speed we roll up some space fabric into a sort of tube around us, and that affects the space fabric for many light years ahead of us."

Bo said, "How did you cut that tunnel?"

The box said, "Plasma, at some thirty thousand degrees centigrade. The space craft that came here thousands of years ago did the same - there had been a space war. The losers fled here, and burrowed far underground. Those pursuers overflew the earth, saw nothing, and went on to search other planets.

"I have asked you a question, and you have not answered, but asked questions instead."

Nicole said, "I'm scared."

Her husband said, "I'm curious."

Nicole said, "I'm more than curious, but …"

Bo said to Anne, "Curiosity killed the cat, but even so..."

Anne said, "Where you go, I follow."

Bo said to the alien, "You see? No input, and she puts it on my shoulders. Do you people have females?"

The alien stood there, immovable.

Fred said, "I don't know your name, but what would you do?"

The box said, "Curiosity is very healthy. I would go."

Fred turned to the others. "He's the guy who knows. He tells us to go."

They nodded unhappily.

PART TWO

They still reeled from the trip on a ship two miles in diameter. The city below had staggered them.

Now, after eating well, and sleeping, they found themselves in a wide, high domed hall, on four chairs facing a table.

Eight figures slowly materialised, and stood behind the table. They were figures of bright, opaque light, each a different color.

The one in the centre was white. It spoke to them directly.

"We are from the most advanced planets in the Confederation. More than a million years ago, we abandoned our bodies of matter for energy fields. If you like, our whole 'bodies' are a form of brain.

"Please let me felicitate you for coming.

"I believe you told our companion in his ship near your moon that you do not believe in God because you can't see him."

Bo folded his arms defensively. "I stand by that."

The other three nodded.

The white mind said, "In our universe, the Holy Spirit is an infinite being, ever swirling, ever moving."

Anne said, "I know the church talks about the Trinity, but I don't understand."

The reddish cloud said, "In heaven, the Godhead is changeless and unchanging. It is infinite, impossible to grasp with our minds. The Godhead has three attributes - love, awareness and will. It willed the Holy Spirit to go out of Itself, substance of His own substance, to create movement. With movement, came time and change and matter. The Holy Spirit's substance, *our* minds can grasp it and *we* dwell in it."

Nicole said calmly, "What I see are galaxies, color; galaxies held together by gravity, but flying away from each other because of Dark Energy."

The blue cloud-mind said, "You come from earth, where your minds are obsessed by me-me-me-me! Your 'me' mind will perish, go down into dust. But God has put into you an indwelling Spirit, of the same substance as God. You have a Spirit indwelling in you, given from the very Hand of God."

They looked dazed.

Anne said, "If I've got a Spirit inside me, it's never made itself known."

The white mind said, "Because your me-me-me mind blinds you to it. Would you accept that you have a consciousness far superior to that of an animal, that your sense of 'me' stays the same all your life?"

Fred barked, "Accepted."

An orange cloud spoke. "Your "me" doesn't exist, and never has; it's an idea fixed in your mind from when you were a child, when adults mirrored you. They mirrored you well or mirrored you ill, so affecting your character. But your 'me' doesn't exist. Your indwelling Spirit gives you a sense of *I AM*, which is impersonal pure consciousness, and which never changes from boy to old man."

Bo said, "I'm aware of 'me' but… well, I guess in a way 'I am' too, now you speak of it."

The figures of light sat considering them.

The white cloud said, "Let us take all this slow step by slow step."

After a silence, the yellow cloud-mind said, "You will accept that you suffer an amazing repertory of emotions. I believe your dictionaries on earth list some two thousand words, each describing an emotion."

The four nodded.

The yellow cloud said, "Let us call that your *inferior channel* for contacting with the world around you. These emotions belong to instincts, neural networks that respond by instinct. You don't make yourself feel the emotions - they are inflicted upon you, out of your control.

"An animal sees danger and feels fear, that drives it to run for its life. The sense of danger is not enough - it is feeling the emotion of fear that lends wings to its heels.

"Your emotions give an enormous force, a tremendous charge to your reactions."

Bo said, "Agreed."

A mauve cloud-mind said, "You also see the world around you through your senses. You see shapes and colors. You feel hardness, cold, heat, sharpness. You taste food. You hear the rustle of a lion, the roar of a tiger. Perhaps you get close enough to smell the lion.

"The world around you is a hologram of the Holy Ghost, which you see with your 2-D retina.

"Your brain joins up the images, the feelings of soft meat, the smell, the taste, the sound of roaring with your sight of a lion, joins them all up, and convinces you that the world *is* out there looking like this and that.

"You agree?"

They nodded.

"Let us call this your *lower seeing*, your *inferior channel*. You trust this level implicitly. If someone tells you that they don't *think* a lion is in the thicket, you're not satisfied. You throw stones into the thicket. If there *is* a lion, it will charge out into the open ground where your spears are poised.

"Can we say that you trust your *lower seeing* as you trust nothing else?"

Bo said, "You can say that again. Now we understand you."

He stared at the luminous mists. They stood about seven feet high, had vague suggestions of a body, arms and legs, with a sort of faceless head on top. He supposed they had adopted that form to make them feel comfortable.

Fred astonished him, by asking, "Do you usually adopt this form, or would you perhaps be in a sphere, say... you know..." he trailed off, uncomfortable.

The reddish one said, "Usually a sphere, but invisible. We expend energy to make ourselves luminous for you."

The white form said, "On to the next thing. You also have minds, intelligence, to reason with. You can use logic with your minds."

They nodded.

"We can call that your *middle seeing*, your *middle bridge* to the outside world, your *middle conduit*. But you do not trust it.

When Einstein used maths to show that time slowed at relativistic speeds, you weren't satisfied till you put an atomic clock in a plane, circling the earth. You had to see the reading on that clock, with your own eyes?"

They nodded.

"Einstein also told you that space curves under gravity. You have had to put four of the most perfect spheres into orbit, to *see* what happens, to satisfy your *lower bridge*, your *lower seeing*. You have to throw those stones into the thicket to make sure there is no lion hiding there?"

They nodded dumbly.

"But your intelligence can't always control your feelings, your passions. Your animal feelings enslave your intelligence to make ever more devastating weapons, to turn your planet into a violent place, with much killing?"

Nicole said, ashamedly, "True."

The orange figure spoke. "You have an indwelling Spirit, come from the very hand of God. To experience that, you must meditate. So you have a *higher bridge*, a *higher seeing*."

Bo said firmly, "We can't accept that. I've never seen anyone do that."

"Ah," said the green mind-mist. "You're confusing your levels. You're asking the *higher seeing* to show itself to the *lower bridge*. You humans have already mixed up the levels by making

Einstein's *middle sight* prove itself on the *lower sight*, on the *lower bridge* with the outside world."

The blue figure said, "When you make a mathematical result, do you always substitute *lower bridge* numbers for your mathematical symbols to see whether the sums come out?"

Fred said sharply, "We already know they will."

The yellow figure said, "So sometimes you accept your middle sight without going to your lower sight, and sometimes you don't?"

No one answered.

The green mind-mist said, "You accept the word of some mathematicians, but not of mystics?"

Anne shrugged. "Who is a mystic? What's a mystic?"

"Your Western religions have neglected the mystics, the Eastern religions have not. But they all speak with the same voice of the glory that is God. So you have no one in high authority to tell you that you can listen to the mystics?"

Bo said, "Fair enough."

Fred said, "Just a minute. Our lower sight is direct experience. The stones, the lions and the spears are *direct* experience. If a tribesman says, 'I'm sure there's no lion in there', he's talking second-hand from his middle level. That way lions can get to eat you.

"Now this higher level, this meditative seeing... what's that? Fifth-hand?"

The white figure said, "It's direct, overwhelming experience, a thousand times more intense than seeing on the lower level."

"Who says so?" said Fred.

The white mind-mist said simply, "I say so."

"But I can't reproduce your experience," said Fred stubbornly.

"Can you reproduce Einstein's math?"

Fred slowly shook his head.

"Yet you accept it, like most humans?"

The white mist asked Anne, "And if at a University cafeteria, you found yourself talking to a History Professor who told you about some Byzantine king you'd never heard of..."

"Yes," said Anne edgily, "I'd accept that."

The blue figure asked them, "How did your science begin?"

Bo grinned delightedly. "That takes us back to school days. The Church taught that heavier objects fell faster than lighter ones. So Galileo climbed the leaning Tower of Pisa and dropped - I dunno, a small cannonball and a big one. They hit the ground together. Next thing, Kepler calculated the proper orbits of the planets, I don't remember. All this in 1600 AD."

"Good," said the white figure. "They looked at nature with

their lower vision, instead of supposing with their middle sight, their middle bridge to the outside world."

Nicole broke in. "You have an amazing knowledge of our planet."

The yellow figure said, "It all came on the ship with you. Kepler found three laws of planetary movement."

The green figure said, "Before Galileo and Kepler, all thought had been philosophic - the middle sight – or meditative - the higher vision. Aristotle, the Greek philosopher, had stared intently at nature, and *classified* what he saw, but did not try to discover anything.

"With Galileo and Kepler, we have a third human - Francis Bacon. He taught *induction* instead of *deduction*. Deduction works while your first idea - the one you are working from - is right, but you can't depend on premises, especially interested ones. Bacon taught you humans to collect a large number of single cases and from them form your law. In deduction, you formulate your law, and get specific instances... but if your law is wrong! Your law proceeds from your middle sight. Induction comes from your lower seeing, your lower bridge to reality. With Francis Bacon, you obviously don't blindly collect pebbles from a river bed - your middle sight asks, what do I want to know?

"Galileo asked his question with his middle mind, and then climbed the Tower of Pisa and got to work with his lower seeing, his senses of his body.

"What Galileo, Kepler and Bacon did was not rational, logical and deductive, from the middle sight. They searched your world with the lower sight, the lower senses, to see whether something happened, or didn't happen. They were looking at change, which is movement in space giving rise to time - which is what the Holy Spirit came forth to create.

"What they taught you was to *measure* the movement, the change - just as time is a measurement of movement, measured by the hands of a clock.

"After Galileo and Kepler came Newton. They all *measured*, and so discovered science. No one discovered science before because no one *measured*. Aristotle taught Western man to *classify*.

"Measurement gave numbers which corresponded to the mathematics of the Holy Ghost, the mathematics of the laws laid down by the Holy Ghost. Aristotle misled humanity - he told them to classify, when he should have told them to *measure* the Holy Ghost's creation. Mathematics are the language of the Holy Ghost in physical creation."

"Hey!" cried Bo, "I see no evidence of the Holy Ghost."

The green mind mist said, "Molecules form matter and form organisms. You agree?"

Bo nodded.

"What makes molecules?"

Bo said, "Atoms."

The green figure said, "Keep going."

"Sub-atomic particles like protons, electrons, neutrons and others make up atoms. Quarks make up protons and neutrons. Strings make up quarks."

"But they all spin? What makes them spin? Why don't they run down?"

All four were silent.

"Because of incredible energy - trillions of trillions of trillions of tons per cubic centimetre pouring into this universe from another dimension and then leaving it. Dimensions are separated by membranes which on Earth you call branes. Why should that energy choose so conveniently to pour into this universe, and then leave it, just in time? The galaxies cling together inside by gravity, but this energy blows them apart. The whole universe is blowing apart."

Bo said, "An accident. Laws of physics."

The white figure said, "This energy comes from God, from the Holy Ghost. It is His Breath. This energy has awareness, His awareness."

"How do you know that?"

"Because we have experienced it directly."

"How can you prove that?"

The white figure said, "Once again, you are confusing

your levels. The middle sight, the middle bridge to reality, the intelligent mind, gives us philosophy, psychology.

"The upper sight is spiritual, is meditative knowledge. You can't mix your levels. Back on earth, your well-meaning Western religion tried to be scientific ('heavier bodies fall faster'), philosophy tried to be religious - the medieval Schoolmen - and science tried to be philosophy.

"You're doing the same.

"Consider your philosopher, Kant. He published his CRITIQUE OF PURE REASON. He saw that the middle level, reason, could not meddle in the contemplative, in the upper sight. He believed in God, in noumenon, which was beyond the bodily senses, the lower seeing, but he also showed that the Ultimate, Transcendental Reality is beyond reason, beyond the middle sight. Why? Because reason can argue for and against the Divine and be right both times, which is nonsense, illogical, absurd. If you cut a sphere down the middle, from top to bottom, you get a circle. Cut the sphere from side to side, and you still get an... identical circle. Place the circles side by side, and they can be vertical or horizontal in the sphere - you can't distinguish.

"Kant said that often language at the middle level of perception could not properly report on the *lower* level either.

"He considered the raw experience at the lower level - your sight of the color of yellow - of experiencing what yellow, yellowness is like.

"At your middle level, you speak or write the word 'yellow', but the word does not convey *yellowness* - would not tell a blind man, or a color-blind person what yellow in flowers or in gold feels like to gaze upon, when seen directly by a normal eye.

"How much less, then, can the middle level, language, talk of the higher spiritual level?

"Philosophers and theologians spout forth on God, using their middle bridge to reality - Kant showed they were talking nonsense. Pure reason cannot seize the Transcendental, the Cloud of Unknowing, the Divine and Eternal Essence.

"Fifteen hundred years earlier, the Buddhist Nagarjuna had said the same, and in the East, the lesson stuck.

"The Christian mystic, Nicholas de Cusa, said that the Ultimate Reality in God enfolds opposites – Buddhism and Hinduism call that *advaya* and *advaita*. Other great Christian mystics echo Nicholas de Cusa.

"Do you have any problem with Nicholas de Cusa?"

Anne said, "We've never heard of him, sorry."

"So you can't accept what he says?"

Nicole said, "If the church preached about that, we would have learned about it."

"Do you go to church?"

"Like most people, I stopped going when I was very young."

Fred said, "I've never been inside a church. My parents never went. But two circles are not necessarily opposites."

"Think then that it is snowing, and not snowing. For your lower, bodily senses, that is surely impossible."

"Impossible," said Fred.

"Then you must forget your lower sight in these matters."

The yellow cloud said, "On your planet, the philosopher A. J. Ayer in his LANGUAGE & TRUTH & LOGIC writes, 'I'm not going to lay down that the mystic can't produce truths by his mystical process... but I do affirm that the mystic does not come up with truths that we can reproduce experimentally... fact is, he doesn't come up with any statements at all which make sense as we understand it.' Or words to that effect.

"I fear he echoes how you four think."

The orange mist mind said, "In the Church, the philosopher of Western mystics, the *Doctor Seraphicus*, St. Bonaventure, taught that humans find knowledge by 'three eyes'; the *carnal eye* which sees space, movement and matter; the *eye of reason* which leads you to philosophy and logic; and the *eye of meditation*, which raises you to God.

"He went further to say that there is outside illumination which lights up the carnal eye; interior illumination which lights up the eye of reason to show the truths of philosophy; and *lumen superius*, the higher illumination which lights up the eye of meditation, which in turn lights up the transcendent Changeless and Unchanging Reality."

The green cloud said, "The Church thrust forth another great mystic; Hugh of St. Victor, who separated out *cogitatio*, *meditatio* and *contemplatio*. Through *contemplatio*, your indwelling Spirit unites with the Godhead, its home.

"*Cogitatio* for Hugh de St. Victor served for seeing matter with the carnal eye.

"*Meditatio* for him was discovering the content of the mind, of the psyche; as distinct from the indwelling eternal Spirit in each of us.

"So these Princes of the Church argued that the carnal eye, the *cogitatio*, the *lumen inferius-exterius*, showed men the low, crass world - the world of matter and movement, movement which gives time. Humans share this world with the higher animals with a like carnal eye. Should a tribesman kill a deer, and a tiger see the man and the deer, the man will find how efficient is the tiger's eye.

"This is the world presented through your 2-D retina. God's hologram is very grainy and sometimes distorted - but the human neurons smooth out the image to perfection.

"This despite the fact that your English philosopher, John Locke, insisted that all knowledge in the mind is first in the five senses.

"The eye of reason, the eye of the mind, the *meditatio*, acts in the realm of ideas, of maths, quarks - in the knowledge that once upon your world lived a Roman emperor called Nero, who has been dead almost two thousand years.

"This middle level has another role - to check your overwhelming surges of emotion and feeling, to stop you from killing, or to make you wait, the better to attack or kill.

"God created early man with an emotional response far richer than any animal. Man had almost no intellectual neurons then. Aliens landed on earth, tampered with his genes, mixed their sperm with human women to produce *homo sapiens sapiens*. They interrupted God's work, and produced an intellect at the service of savage emotional circuits. Read *Genesis*.

"They did not wipe out the emotions, the feelings first.

"Today, your planet has a black record - of violence, killing, of rich and needy… your psyches are split.

"The earlier man lived in a Garden of Eden, till the serpent from space changed him. In olden times, serpents were invariably symbols for space ships, with their fiery tails.

"God's prehistorical man lived in a magic, spiritual world. He could not talk, or had very few words at his command. His limited sense of self was at one with the tribe, with nature and with God.

"Today's individuality did not exist. They merged into each other, into nature, and into God, because for them nature was mystical, God's very own Garden of Eden."

Anne cried, "Why didn't God repair the damage?"

The white cloud said, "God gives us all free will. And now you are dearer to God than those on sane planets, in your suffering and unending mistakes. You are very special to Him now, in all your evil."

Bo asked, "What is *evil*, damn it?"

The blue cloud said, "Evil is separation from God. Evil is separation or denial of love."

Fred said, "We understand that *homo sapiens sapiens* came from evolutionary changes. This talk of spacemen is a bit hard to swallow."

Nicole broke in, "Serpents! The ships we saw, and that brought us here are discs."

The reddish cloud said, "The craft of those warring spacemen, who were escaping, their crafts were tubular, long and thin, and produced an extended tail of blazing chemicals to land and take off."

The white mind-mist said, "How can you talk such muddy nonsense about evolution? Humans have thousands of millions of bits of DNA. Only some three percent codes for flesh and bone; the rest supervises. How many babies are born monsters or deformed? Amazingly few.

"To change a hominid to another hominid form needs unbelievably prodigious work. You have to know your sequences of amino acids - what proteins they will form. You have to know how the molecules will open and shut, or deform, when faced by other proteins.

"If you manage the three percent, you have to modify

the supervising DNA in its millions of bits to accept the new sequences, and not delete them.

"The problem is not only proteins. It is the molecules to form them. You have to know the molecules.

"Then the whole creature has to be consistent. Knees ... hips ... spine... neck... head. This is what the Holy Spirit does.

"The spacemen on earth took a short cut - they modified their sperm so the sperm could penetrate the human ova. Then they waited to see whether this gave them a monster, or a viable baby, a viable adult.   In this, they defied the Holy Spirit."

The blue cloud said, "The first creation of life - forms on uncounted planets were wrought by angels, whom the Holy Spirit guided. Angels created some advanced intelligences, who then wrought - or wreaked - their own life-forms."

Anne said, "I'm sorry, we're Darwinists and evolutionists. Spacemen coming and changing life forms on our earth! Rubbish!"

The yellow cloud said, "On our planet here, we have hundreds of thousands of professors whose favorite way of spending their time is to tinker with new life forms. They usually make five males and five females - each with slight genetic changes. One pair alone would bring forth clones only.

"They keep them here to breed - see if they breed true. When their breeding brings their number up to about thirty, the doting professor carries them to one planet or another, and finds as safe a place as he can to leave them."

The orange cloud said, "Only half a dozen could be wiped out."

Anne said, more conciliatory, "Do you know who those 'gods' were, in Genesis, in the Bible, who found the daughters of men so fair?"

The orange cloud said, "A planet of our Confederation."

Bo snorted. "And what about all the flesh-devourers, all the stinging insects, all the nasties?"

"Aliens from another planet, not accepted into our Confederation. Their enjoyments take a vicious turn."

There was a long silence.

Bo asked, more calmly, "How many planets are in the Confederation?"

The green cloud said, "About eight thousand. These are far advanced planets, with a technology humans would find incredulous."

Fred said, "It's incredulous enough that we have come ten million light-years in three days."

The orange cloud said, "We could give you a camera to photograph the night sky. Back on earth, if you showed that photo to an astronomer, he could tell you how far you are from your solar system. But then you would betray yourselves… and us.

"Do you believe me when I say where you are now?"

The four looked doubtful. Bo said, "We need proof."

The orange cloud said, "To convince your lower seeing, your carnal eye? Suppose I tell you that in the Milky Way we have about 300 billion stars."

Anne said, "Well, I believe you."

"You could check back on earth?"

"That too. How many galaxies are there in our universe?"

"About a million million. Do you believe that?"

Bo said, "Why not? It's a number we could check."

The green cloud said, "You mean, you could check the number back on Earth. Why would you believe your informant on Earth?"

"It would depend what university he was from, and his ranking in his field."

The blue cloud said, "Now your information depends on a university and on ranking. How far are you going with that?"

The white cloud said, "Suppose I tell you that you live in an electromagnetic haze and in spinning whorls of particles. Your senses relay that to your brain, which creates a smooth, technicolor image?"

Bo said, "It could be."

"On your earth, some mathematicians have shown this."

"Ah!" exclaimed Bo. "Well, that's it."

"You believe your mathematicians before you believe us. Yet we know how to carry you ten million light years in three days."

"That's all unfamiliar, confusing," muttered Anne, defensively.

The green cloud said, "Suppose I tell you that God dwells in the eternal Present, but we can't experience it here in the cosmos. We are full of the Past and Future, which don't exist.

"We can't *feel* the Present because change flows through it without end. Matter stays in the Present for only one millionth trillionth trillionth trillionth of a second.

"It doesn't flow through the present smoothly, but goes tic-toc. It materialises in the cosmos, then vanishes, then comes back.

"Because it is not real.

"There are a million trillion trillion trillion ticks a second."

"Do they know that on earth?" asked Nicole.

"Your mathematicians have found it."

Bo said, "I accept that."

The white cloud said, "Because of the numbers?"

Bo said defensively, "Numbers change everything."

A beige cloud which had not yet spoken said, "And on earth, the scientists with their numbers give the peoples of the western countries toys of every sort - cars, jumbo jets, electrical machines, electronic ones. They fill their bellies, while the rest of the world is needy, if not hungry and ill.

Thanks to their middle level, middle sight. The peoples call these scientists their gods, and learn from them to count too – but they count money unceasingly."

The four from earth sat stoney-faced.

To try to steer the conversation Nicole said, "I can't believe this of the gods and human women... spacemen."

The mauve colored cloud said, "Read Erich von Däniken, his THE GOLD OF THE GODS, with its photos to convince your lower sight. Listen to his arguments, to convince your middle sight, your middle mind's eye."

The beige cloud said, "We were talking about Kant, who showed that the middle bridge, pure reason, only leads us to paradox when it tries to understand God. What he showed, and Wittgenstein too, was that the metaphysical taken at the middle level, that of understanding by the mind, was balderdash, senseless. The propositions are not wrong, they are meaningless.

"We come back to errors of level, the miring up of levels. Pure reason cannot behold God, nor peer into eternity. You must open the higher sight, the higher eye, as Nagarjuna taught

- pranja - to see God directly, without any thought or word or understanding.

"Kant showed you humans that pure reason couldn't do that because of the very nature of reason, of the middle way."

The mauve cloud said, "But in short decades after Kant's death, humans were dazzled by Newton, and thought the lower way, the lower sight of the five senses alone would lead them to ultimate knowledge. Auguste Comte plunged the West into scientism – that is, man had to trust the lower way, which now carried on its back the middle and higher ways.

"Confusion of levels carried to an extreme. The scienticians said the lower eye could see for all three eyes.

"How sorely have you paid for that on Earth."

The white cloud said, "We have seen how rooted are our four friends here in the lower way. You feel you are keeping your feet firmly on the ground, are you not?"

No one answered him. After a long silence, Bo said, "With our feet on the ground we know where we are. We get results. We build planes, as you say, and don't go hungry."

The green cloud said, "Science stands solidly on the lower bridge, on the lower sight. With that we do not quarrel.

"But it has to shuffle onto the middle level to build a plane – that of reason. But reason will never tell you whether a lion lies crouched in the thicket or not. You must throw stones.

"You always come back to saying, 'What the lower eye doesn't see we don't know for sure. We have a surefire way of finding out by our five senses. Quarks are probably there, but we still ain't seen one…!' The middle level MUST BE CHECKED by the lower.'

"And from there, you have taught humans to think that what science hasn't found out … well, it's dicey what it still hasn't found. Galileo, Kepler and Newton showed you that questions could be settled beyond doubt, and that sent philosophers and theologians reeling. They couldn't climb up the Leaning Tower of Pisa to confirm the proof of our Very God, verify, authenticate Him as the Absolute Ground of the cosmos and of our being.

"Galileo, Kepler and Newton did not use their *lumen superius* but scaled higher and higher peaks without it, culminating in Newton's *Principia*.

"Einstein went further, but what matters to the ordinary man in the West today is Newton - his laws keep the jumbo jets in the air and help send space probes to Mars.

"Even Kant succumbed to Newton. He had wanted to be a physicist anyway, not a philosopher, and this undermined much of his philosophy, despite his success with the Critique of Pure Reason.

"Philosophers bowed down to the new scientism. Flint wrote, 'The true method of metaphysics is fundamentally the same as that which Newton has introduced into natural science, and which has there given such fruitful results.'

"How your planet has paid for those words. Because with each new blinding success of science, the more the middle and higher ways shrank, grew more faded and desiccated.

"In scientism, humans not only strayed from God, but strayed from thought that didn't have its feet firmly on the ground. Feet on the ground usually meant measurement.

"Now, understand that we are talking about checking not by personal experience in general but checking by lower senses. And the lower senses cannot check mystical meditation.

"That ruled out not only the higher meditative sight but philosophical searches and thinking at the middle sight, in the middle mind. They did not say, what the lower senses can't see, they can't see; they were saying that what the lower sight could not see, that did not exist. Wittgenstein said plainly enough, 'Whereof one cannot speak, therefore one must be silent.'

"But the advanced lands of your planet were now saying, 'Whereof you can't speak, that's not there.'"

The beige mind-mist said, "Kant believed in the Eternal Being and showed you can't reach it by the lower senses nor by the middle scientific reasoning."

"The philosophers who followed him carried the western planet into darkness... Ayer, Flew, Quine today, and before them, Comte and Mach. They shut their minds against the higher sight of meditation, and gave themselves wholly over to the lower sight of the carnal senses... like our four friends here."

Fred said, "Show us God! Here! Show us!"

The beige cloud said, "The caveman cried, 'Build me a jet plane. Now! Here!'"

Fred scowled.

The mauve mist said, "No knowledge other than that of the lower carnal senses became admissable. The middle bridge - the upper bridges of God, Christ, Buddha, Braham and Tao were gabble, rodomontade. As Ken Wilbur wrote in EYE TO EYE, 'As scientism couldn't measure God it said God was absurd and made no sense. So Christ fantasied, Buddha was schizo, Krishna deluded, Lao Tzu was a mental case.' I am paraphrasing him, but that was his gist."

Anne asked, "Who was Quine?"

The yellow cloud, said, "H. Smith, in his THE FORGOTTEN TRUTH, tells us, 'that for him Williard Quine carried more weight than any other philosopher in the last 20 years.' I paraphrase, as always. He wrote that in 1976.

"Your philosophers published interesting things in recent times, especially since about your year of 1950. L. Whyte in his THE NEXT DEVELOPMENT OF MAN wrote that the lower sight, 'disorganised your personality in that instead of the subject dominating the object, for you the object now holds sway over the subject'. My words, of course."

The white cloud said, "And threw western humans into a Godless darkness."

The yellow cloud went on, "H. Smith, in his FORGOTTEN TRUTH, wrote, 'Science ignores values because it can't measure them... values, meanings and final ends in our lives are lost like seawater flows through a fisherman's net.' Or words like that." He fell silent.

The blue cloud finally said, "A. N. Whitehead in his SCIENCE AND THE MODERN WORLD says that the system you have on earth is that 'every university is organised by our lower sight. No one has any other way to suggest. So this way reigns without any contender. I can't believe it.' Or words to that effect."

The red cloud looked at each of the four.

"UNBELIEVABLE!"

The blue cloud went on, "Thomas McPherson writes in RELIGION AS THE INEXPRESSIBLE, 'Because you can check what a scientist claims, one can only measure sense by other sense experiences, and where you can't even do that, then you're into the ridiculous.' To paraphrase. Elsewhere, he warns that religion enters into the 'unutterable.'

"N. O. Brown, in his LIFE AGAINST DEATH, tells all you humans that, 'the problem isn't the lay-out of science but the unconscious lay-out of the scientific mind...Whitehead called today's scientific viewpoint as quite unbelievable.' Brown goes on to say 'take psychoanalysis - insane.'"

The reddish cloud said, "What is more insane, than coming here to tell us that your life on earth arose from the mud, and evolves on its own. Darwin! What insanity!"

Nicole said nervously, "We haven't said that..."

The reddish mind-mist said, "Not yet. Remember, we can read your minds. We know that you think and believe that madness."

The yellow cloud said, "L. Whyte, in his THE NEXT DEVELOPMENT OF MAN, tells you that 'every magnitude has equal standing in the laws of elementary arithmetic' Or some such words. 'So anything not arithmetical just isn't there. God? Nothing! Your cars and motorbikes, with tolerances of a thousandth of an inch, make your cities hell – streets frightening and polluted."

The green cloud said, "Whitehead tells you that 'if you ignore science, you bring down wrath on your head. Science has mutated into scientific materialism.'

"Look what progress scientific materialism has given you humans in the West in the last five hundred years - see the killing today, the inequality, the hunger all over the world. How you Westerners gobble up the wealth. God and the angels weep."

The orange cloud said, "As Whitehead further says, 'All we have left is a stark lack of values... they push our gaze today to things, seldom to values.' My words."

The white cloud said, "Whitehead also says in his SCIENCE AND THE MODERN WORLD, 'Dress it up as you will, the scientific philosophy of the end of the seventeenth century has brought us to... nature is drab, cheerless, colorless, soundless, no scents, just the flurry of matter, unending, without significant design.'"

The yellow cloud went on, "Like the endless, meaningless hurry of your cars, of your planes, of all your toys. Philosophy and science are now antagonists on your planet. As J. J. Van der Leeuw says in his THE CONQUEST OP ILLUSION, 'Mutual contempt of philosophy is as harmful as it is unfounded.'

Whitehead is definite and final on that. He says, 'Thereby modern philosophy has been ruined.'

"And what do our four visitors say?"

Anne said, "Let's face it, philosophy is speculation."

The white mist said, "The middle bridge, the middle sight? No feet on the ground?"

Fred exploded, "Oh? come on! Philosophy has no feet on the ground! It's got its head up in the clouds. Today, we live at a good standard of living. If we want to go to the Gobi desert to look at fossils, we have jets that will take us there! What did philosophy ever make fly? It couldn't keep a piece of paper up in the air."

The beige cloud said, "As psychiatrist Karl Stern tells you in E. Schumacher's A GUIDE FOR THE PERPLEXED, 'It's madness to think like that. And I mean *mad*. Psychotic, that is,' or something like that."

Silence fell.

The yellow mind-mist said, "Michio Kaku is a physicist famed planet-wide. He published HYPERSPACE, and in VOICES OF TRUTH, he says, 'They used to declare that what you can measure is all you get. That's the damaging bias that physicists have - there's nothing beyond. If they can't measure it, it's not in reality.'"

The blue cloud said, "Willard Quine's influence has been immense. Huston Smith says, 'To sum up, in Quine's world there's only one sort of essence of physical bodies in our world that natural scientists study. Physical wholes or parts. There's only one sort of learning in our world - it's the knowledge only scientists have.'"

The beige cloud, said, "William James tried to tell his fellow man. He wrote in his THE VARIETIES OF RELIGIOUS EXPERIENCE that, 'Usually when we're awake, we think of this as our normal mind, but it is only one very particular sort of consciousness: the fact is that all around us, hidden by the thinnest of fragile veils, of masks, lies every different sort of mind states.'

"The higher bridges, the higher meditation."

The white mind-mist said, "It is not altogether displeasing that this planet lies ten million light-years away."

The beige cloud said, "Down the ages, they have had insights. Their New Testament warns, 'What does it serve a man to gain the whole world if he loseth his own soul?'"

The white cloud said, "We could not have put it better."

The beige cloud said, "The Hindu *Upanishads* are very good. This was written thousands of their years ago:

> 'The eye goes not there,
>
> Speech goes not, nor the mind.
>
> We know it not, we understand it not.'

"The third higher sight perfectly expressed.

"Another Upanishad says:

> 'From the not-real lead me to the real!
>
> From darkness, show me light!
>
> From death lead me to immortality!'

"Earthmen, is that not beautiful?"

Fred said, "Everyone wants to be immortal, but dust we are and to dust do we return."

The orange cloud said, "Beyond the lower and middle bridges, the higher sight leads us to Eternity, to immortality - the higher eye of our indwelling Spirit, given us from the hand of God. Listen to this Upanishad:

> 'You cannot hear it, touch it;
>
> Without form, everlasting;
>
> Nor can you taste it, smell it,
>
> It is never ending;
>
> Without beginning, without end,
>
> Higher than the highest, Immutable -

By seeing That, you are freed from the mouth of death.'"

The blue cloud said, "The Upanishads tell you:

'He who, dwelling in all things,

Yet is other than all things,

Whom the things know not,

Whose Body all things are,

Who controls the cosmos from within -

He is your Soul, your Inner Spirit,

God the Immortal.'"

The yellow cloud commented, "For you earthmen, numbers are all. But something can be better than another; a number can't. Will you accept that love is better than violence, yet four is not better than seven."

Fred joked, "If they are dollars…"

"I'm not talking about *things* but pure numbers. And your planet with its philosophy of measurements and numbers has been left without qualities. A stronger country invades a weaker; a weaker nation cannot attack a stronger. Ethics, morality… where are they on that planet of yours?"

Bo asked, "So what are values?"

"If we consider values, then the higher meditative sight is more vital than the middle mind bridge, which is in turn more precious than the lower carnal sight. Why? Because the Being of God imbues the higher meditation, the higher vision.

"What do you recognise? That a bigger jumbo jet is better than a 24-seater feeder prop-driven Fokker? The astronomical distance you have travelled to come here is better than the distance a modest earth-probe travels to try and land on Mars without crashing? That the gross national product of Germany is bigger and better than that of Luxembourg? Are these not lower, materialist, carnal values on a level almost with the animals?

"Is it cleverer to probe into the *smaller* zoo of subatomic particles, than into the larger *macroscopic* world of mechanical engineering?"

Nicole said, "Now you're being rude. That is not fair. We can't argue philosophy."

The white cloud said, "Well, we shall try to teach you a little philosophy. Understand, then, that modern science has not only changed your life in western countries out of recognition, but it has warped your thinking and culture, how you see yourself in the world.

"Last century, when you found the universe was infinitely bigger than you first thought, when you found the zoo of subatomic particles, you got a shock. Newton's physics worked for your engines and planets, but not for the universe.

"The new picture of the universe came closer to that knowledge held by the mystics, Western and Eastern, but especially Eastern. As the father of the atom bomb said, more or less: 'Our general ideas of atomic physics are not entirely novel. We see those ideas in Buddhist and Hindu thinking; in fact, they are central to that thinking.' He wrote that in his book, SCIENCE AND UNDERSTANDING; he was a Sanskrit scholar.

"On your planet, the two fountains of your physics are quantum theory and relativity. Both look at the world in the way the Hindus, Buddhists and Taoists do. In the East, spiritual philosophies there are in huge number, but mystically inclined philosophies all over your world have this view - a view found through your higher vinculum, your higher bridge to Reality. The Christian mystics here join with the Greek mystical philosophers. The weighty difference is that in your Western religion, mysticism rarely entered the sermons from the church pulpits. In the East, the mystical schools are central."

The beige mind-mist said, "Some 2500 years ago, in the sixth century BC, the early Greek philosophers were mystical, but they turned away from that, leading you to the world you live in today.

"In Greece, in that sixth century BC we find not only mysticism but the roots of your planet's physics. For those Greeks, religion, science and philosophy were intertwined. In the Milesian School, in Iona, they sought 'physis', the underlying reality of everything, and your word 'physics' today comes from 'physis'.

"The Milesians were mystical - they called them 'hylozoists' which is to say that they thought matter *lived*, as we know it does."

The four from earth laughed outright.

The beige cloud said, "It lives and it does not. It is true to say that, and it is not. Your lower and middle bridges to the world outside of you cannot grasp it. Your higher sight can. Remember, the Godhead was utterly still, Perfect in Love, in Awareness and Will, and It did will what you call the Holy Ghost to go forth from itself, God substance of God substance, to create movement - and with movement, He created change and time. In this universe, what he put into movement were vibrating strings which gave rise to quarks and atomic particles. These form into every conceivable matter, with beginnings and ends, but His energy sustains all, His Living Breath imbues the smallest and the greatest.

"Hear this. The Milesians didn't even have a word for matter since they saw every palpable form disclosed alive with spirituality - as it *is*. Alive with the breath of the Holy Spirit. Thales and Anaximander saw the universe as full of gods, or as 'breathing', alive by *pneuma*, the cosmic breath.

"Here we find thinking that comes together with the ancient Chinese and Indians; and Heraclitus of Ephesus drew yet nearer to those in the East. He saw a world of 'Becoming', which is true because the Holy Spirit creates unceasingly. He saw static Being as a delusion of our senses, and the Holy Ghost is not static."

The mauve cloud said, "This unsullied intuition from their higher sight was not to last. The new Eleatic School broke off on a new line. They taught a Divinity in a lofty abode high above mankind - a clever and personal God, orchestrating the world.

"The first step towards splitting apart spirit and matter, which today is your Western thinking, on your planet.

"Parmenides from Elea set his face against Heraclitus. He postulated an immutable Being, and the change we see all about us as an illusion - our senses fall into a trap. From this Greek, you get your idea of invariable substances thrusting forth all the appearances... except he said the appearances were delusory.

"In the West, you teach the conservation of energy, the lasting strings giving lasting quarks, which give lasting protons. An atom can mutate into another one with radioactive decay, but protons are forever.

"Atoms in the molecules give you the multifaceted world you live in.

"In the fifth century BC, the Greeks tried to smooth over the struggle between Parmenides and Heraclitus. Two men, Leucippus and Democritus came up with the atom, and sharply separated spirit and matter. Matter was the unending permutations of these basic building atoms... dead atoms, ever moving.

"What moved the atoms? They could not explain that, but allowed a spiritual energy, completely apart from matter.

"That set the stage for your Western world today - mind against matter, body against soul, that any greengrocer, taxi-driver or brick-layer accepts unthinkingly.

"So, the philosophers turned to the spiritual and ethical. The Western Churches of the Middle Ages followed the spiritual quest, and science languished until your Renaissance, when men shook off the Church, when Galileo, Kepler and Newton stepped into history.

"The midwife at the birth of your modern science carried your thinking to extremes in the split between mind and matter. In the seventeenth century, the philosopher Rene Descartes divided the world into *res cogitans*, the lower and middle bridges; and *res extensa*, inert matter.

"Descartes taught scientists to think of matter as dead, and you inhabited a mental world from the seventeenth century to the end of the nineteenth that was a clockwork Newtonian universe of utterly unbreakable natural laws imposed by a kingly God reigning far above you.

"Descartes' famous words were '*Cogito ergo sum*', '*I think, therefore I exist*' led you Westerners to equate your existences with the mind, with your middle sight, and to see your egos, your me-me-me-me as lonely entities inside your bodies.

"The truth is that '*I have an indwelling Spirit, therefore I exist,*' an indwelling Spirit accessible through your higher meditation, your higher awareness.

"Worse, you see the world around you fragmented into countless things and happenings, all outside you, all inert and dead, yours for the taking. So today you live on a planet of crass inequality, cruel economic disruption and pollution, hunger, sickness and death, with violence and killing on all sides. This is living like subhumans, at an animal level."

"You deny your highest level. Very few humans have travelled in space. Does the rest of humanity say it's impossible? Yet you say the mystics journeys are."

The orange cloud said, "In Eastern mysticism, all is interwoven, all are projections of the Ultimate. To see ourselves as lonely egos is for them an illusion, product of your minds that measure and classify. The Buddhists call it *avidya* or ignorance. But today, East and West are equally rapacious.

"'For the turbulent mind, multiplicity;

For the serene mind, multiplicity vanishes.'

"But the Buddhist, Hindu and Taoist teach you to lose your solitary self and open your eyes to the interwoven unity about you. What you see as dead objects, they say are ever-flowing, ever-changing, ever-moving, organic and alive: spirit in matter and matter in spirit.

"They deny the classical Greek view that energy is outside matter, 'pushing it from the outside', but is within, as your modern physics would agree. They say that not a Divinity, on high, conducts movement and change from afar, but a Divine breath infuses all from within.

"As the Upanishad says:

'He who, abiding in everything,

Yet is Other than all things.'"

The blue cloud said, "Understand that you perceive an electromagnetic hologram with your 2-D retina. Two thousand years ago, the Hindu Tantras told us that reality is an illusion, that the seer and the seen are one. Your philosopher, Alfred Whitehead, also wrote of cloudy reality:

> 'What I contest is to divide nature into two -
> namely, nature as we know through our awareness
> and the nature which excites and animates that
> awareness. We are sensible, alert to how green are
> the trees, the singing of birds, the warming sun, the
> sturdiness of chairs, the feel of velvet.
>
> Nature which awakens our awareness, which
> activates a supposed system of molecules and
> electrons in our brains to produce awareness is
> considered another sort.'

"He wrote that in his THE CONCEPT OF NATURE... or words to that effect.

"Your quantum physicist Werner Heisenberg has given you his Uncertainty Principle, which says that the seer changes the seen by merely watching. In his PHYSICS AND PHILOSOPHY he wrote, 'outside reality dissolved into mathematics which no longer give so much the behaviour of elementary particles as our perception of this behaviour.' Or some such words.

"Your old physics talked of a world outside of you of hard matter, sticks and stones and bones. Natural laws were final.

"Now physicists are telling you that the hologram of

the electromagnetic mist out there is susceptible to your consciousness.

"In the old physics, any scientist could duplicate a successful and recognised experiment, because it was always the same universe out there with fixed laws.

"Today, you are not sure that when you repeat an experiment the same result will come out. You cannot count on fixed laws - the consciousness of the experimenter can change the result.

"You can't observe the universe as before, because there are too many of them."

Fred cried incredulously, "Different dimensions!"

The white cloud said, "How do you think you came here in three days, travelling at 120,000 times the speed of light. You went through the branes enfolding this universe into other dimensions."

Nicole said heatedly, "If we are ten million light-years away."

The reddish cloud said, "It appears we must abduct an astronomer too."

The white cloud said, "You saw our ship at the moon was 100 miles across. That is because we have an accelerator ring inside the outside edge, more than 300 miles long. That is to break through the brane into the Tachyon universe you travelled in.

"Some branes are easy, but this one is extraordinarily difficult.

"The 100 mile ship with you inside broke through, and we launched your ship. Here, another ship awaited you in that dimension, to break back into this universe.

"Sometimes, a ship of 50 yards across and an accelerator ring of 150 yards can break through certain branes, if it is light enough has practically no mass."

The blue cloud said, "The trouble is that we have brought you to the point where your language no longer gives you any information. Metaphysics got there an age ago. In the late 1800s, your Charles Dodgson, a mathematician in England, saw mathematically different dimensions, branes. So, writing under the name of Lewis Carrol, he wrote *Alice in Wonderland* and *Alice through the Looking Glass*, pushing language to its very limits. The Looking Glass was the brane… Alice crossed into a dimension where things were and were not. The Cheshire Cat vanished leaving just its Grin. The Queen was 2-D - the Queen of playing cards. Alice got bigger, got smaller. The rabbit was late, was late… Common sense was senseless and animals talked in paradoxes.

"You are far from other dimensions at your level on your planet. You are a long way from 10^{19} billion electron volts you need to break through a brane, while our Confederation has many planets that control the Planck energy.

"One hundred years ago, Auguste Compte said humans would never reach the stars and never know what they are made of. For you today, higher dimensions, lower dimensions, time travel, 'beam me up, Scotty' are absurdities."

The beige cloud said, "You idolise dead space and matter as the final, definite, permanent universe out there, chained in the natural laws the Holy Spirit, The Right Hand of God, proclaimed. But what the Holy Spirit can tie, the Right Hand of God unties.

"Mystics have told you over and again that Reality is impalpable. All your ideas of the fixed universe out there are wrong. You even think that dead matter is a universe so complete that it can evolve creatures and men to higher levels. That is childish.

"Your Heisenberg said, 'The violent reaction to modern physics... (comes from)... the feeling that the ground would be cut from science.'[2]

"Everett-Wheeler have shown that quantum theory allows for every possible result to an experiment, in an indefinite number of parallel realities. This doesn't make sense to you. What does it mean? Language can't tell you, as the language can't help you in your higher contact with Reality. Words are the girders that underpin your middle bridge to the world outside, but that is for your middle and lower contacts."

The mauve cloud said, "You must think that you live in a world of ten dimensions, with tiny strings vibrating in those dimensions. The Greeks - Pythagoras - thought that violin strings were an allegory for how the universe works. They said that violin strings reflected the universal harmonies.

---

2   *Physics and Philosophy* (Harper Torchbooks)

"Your Murray Gell-Mann, who won the Nobel Prize for finding the quark, said the simplest image of the quark was that of a vibrating string.

"When the physicist Michio Kaku was at University, he tells us that he asked his professor, 'What is light?'

"'Why, it's wave'.

"'If light's waving in a vacuum, it means nothing is waving. How can nothing wave?'

"The professor told him he had to take his word for it.

"Now Kaku says that what's waving is what mystics call the fifth dimension."

Nicole said, dazed. "Ten dimensions!"

The orange cloud said, "If you push a rod through a sheet of paper, a flatlander would draw a circle there, and think he'd got your rod. You'd just pull the rod back out.

"Kaku said, 'If a flatlander puts his gold in a safe, and thinks it is hidden, you could see it from your third dimension, and grab it.'

"God, from a higher dimension, can see all. We can hide nothing. And living in the eternal, changeless Present, he can see past and future in an instant."

Bo said, "I can't visualise other dimensions beyond the three we live in."

The reddish cloud said, "You evolved to shin up trees when

you saw a cave-bear or an angry mammoth. God had no more in mind for you then."

"Where are the branes?" asked Anne.

"Touching our universe at every point," said the white cloud. "The space craft that brought you here can cross branes from where it lies moored."

"Show us other dimensions," Fred demanded.

The reddish mind-mist said, "Nichio Kaku said that the dimensions ripple and we can see the ripples. The ripples give us light, the strong nuclear force holding atoms together - he says they make the stars shine. You don't have to believe us. Kaku has impeccable university qualifications on your planet. He says that when the fifth dimension vibrates, you get light. When the sixth, seventh and eighth dimensions vibrate, you get Yang-Mill fields. They are the glue - the gluons - that hold the quarks together, which no force can separate except an exploding supernova star."

Bo asked dazedly, "Are there other dimensions too?"

The blue light said, "On your planet, at the beginning of the twentieth century, an Indian called Ramanujan worked as a postal clerk… one of the greatest mathematicians your world has seen. Without training, without contact with Europe, alone he derived about two hundred of European mathematical postulates. In 1913, he wrote a letter to Godfrey Hardy, an outstanding Cambridge mathematician, and Hardy couldn't believe what he was seeing.

"Hardy used to rate mathematicians from one to hundred; he put himself at 30 and Ramanujan at 100. He brought Ramanujan to England, where the climate would kill him of tuberculosis.

"But for some years the two produced a hurricane of mathematical formulae, the most famous being the Ramanujan Function... an elliptic modular function that operates only in 24 dimensions. He found that 8 and 24 dimensions were stable - any other number crumbles down to three or down to eight... in physics, it is 10 and 26, and in maths it is 8 and 24."

"Another universe is out there in 26 dimensions?" Fred asked.

"It is too soon for you humans to know. Ramanujan used his higher, mystical eye to enter into other dimensions, and brought back what he found.

"In quantum physics, the electron can be in many states at once, because it is in parallel universes."

Anne said, "But the branes separating universes are like solid sheets?"

"The branes are like a porous mesh, full of holes the size of a centimeter divided by 10^{33} - that is, ten to the power of 33 zeros, which is a billion trillion trillion. But you must remember Heisenberg's Uncertainty Principle. The hole can grow big enough to swallow a man at any time - that is why on your Earth you have stories of men in the middle of a field suddenly vanishing."

Bo said, "But with the proper energy, you can burst through?"

"The least energy you would need is a billion electron volts multiplied by 10^{19} - that is, a total of a hundred million trillion electron volts."

Nicole asked, "How many other dimensions are there? What are they like?"

The reddish cloud said, "Uncounted other dimensions. Some are universes parallel to ours, but in our past, or in our future. In others, the choices you have made in this universe, abandoning other choices, change. You live a different life there. Where you took a left-hand fork here, you take the right-hand one there.

"Other universes are other forms of life, or hold different, prodigious energies."

Bo said narrowly, "So if the branes are porous, those dimensions leak into ours?"

The orange mind mist said, "Yes."

Bo said, "But what are the laws of physics to do this!"

The white mind mist said, "Laws! Do you think you live in a clockwork universe, where a cog on one wheel pushes the next wheel? Do you think that everywhere two straight parallel lines never meet? Parallel lines on a sphere are curved, as they are on a concave saddle.

"Back in the eighteen hundreds, your mathematician Georg

Riemann proposed a geometry that NO line is ever parallel to the first line. Einstein used Riemannian geometry for his theory of Relativity.

"Einstein showed that you live in a universe where time meanders and flows at different speeds among the galaxies and through the Dark Energy - that time eddies and swirls.

"You imagine that some unknown laws of physics transform mud into a human being. Where are those laws! You have not discovered a single one, because they don't exist. You worship a minor scientist of considerable ignorance called Darwin!

"Know this! You are dwelling in the creation of the Holy Ghost. The perfect Will and perfect Awareness of the Right Hand of God has created all the dimensions so that your lower and middle awareness may learn, so that your divine Spirit abiding with you may learn, and go back to heaven with all it has learnt.

"The Lord your God in the Cosmos is a God of unbelievably huge energies and forces, Who is aware of each particle, Who is closer to you than you are to yourself. He has created all the dimensions so that you can see your life in this world, then pass to other worlds and see what might have been, what you might have done."

Fred snapped, "We can't cross the branes!"

"One day, you will be able to. But know now that each red corpuscle racing through your blood vessels - the Holy Ghost put it there, and guides what it does.

"Natural laws! The Holy Spirit has written natural laws which He breaks according to his perfect Will. Trillions of worlds has He created. You are not your bodies, your lower and middle Eyes, your senses, your brains and your minds! You are your eternal Spirits which will depart when your body, brain and mind dies. You are the very sons of God, your Spirits of God-substance, eternal, immortal, imperishable from the Beginning when the Godhead willed your Spirits out of his Being and gave them free will to roam heaven and the worlds, to roam the perishable dimensions of Creation.

"You live in the perishable realm, in the kingdom of the Most High, perfect in love."

The silence lengthened, and lengthened.

Fred said finally, "I'd like to ask a question. What about reincarnation on our planet? Is that for real?"

The yellow mind-mist said, "On earth, you have Dr. Ian Stevenson, who is Chairman Emeritus of the Department of Psychiatry at the University of Virginia. He and his helpers have studied more than 2,000 children with memories of their previous life. Children remember; then the memory dies away.

"Some thousands reincarnate, and those usually remember the previous life in their early years. The children talk about it, and the news travels wide.

"The Buddhists say reincarnation takes a thousand years, but usually it is about one hundred years. Where death was violent, or where children died very young - they come back much more quickly.

"With violent death, Stevenson and his helpers have catalogued a high percentage of birthmarks at the place where the bullet, the spear, the knife and so on entered the body. Children sometimes remembered a mortal stroke to the head - and when they asked permission to look, they often found birthmarks on the scalp at the very place, but hidden by the hair. The children didn't know they had that birthmark hidden as it was under the hair.

"Many of these children showed xenoglossy - they could speak a foreign language they had never heard of in their present life.

"Normally, the inner Spirit does not intervene with the brain, but in these cases it does, the better for the children to learn. What is the same is the inner Spirit. The child is a new entity, told of the life of another."

Anne said, "Those who seek inward with their higher... er, mind... er, their higher eye - is there a psychical field their psychic search excites?"

"Yes, there is a field, with particles that can travel at any speed, and time is relative, because the field acts in the Present."

Bo said, "It seems to me that scientists stick with science back home, and don't get involved with this mystic stuff."

The white mind mist said, "You are in a considerable error. I will tell you about Sir James Jeans, who was born on your planet in 1877 and died in 1946. He told you that ALL the pictures which your science tries to paint of nature and come closest to the truth with are mathematical ones.

"He said that most scientists would concur they are fictional portrayals because your science did not touch the final reality. That what the twentieth century philosophy stood out for was not relativity from Einstein, quanta from De Broglie, Planck, Heisenberg and Schrödinger, which denies cause and effect, with their cutting up of the atom to show nothing is what it seems to be - but the facing up to the fact that your science has not reached ultimate reality.

"He goes on to talk about Plato's cave - that mankind is inside a cave with their backs to the world outside. You can only study the shadows on the walls of the cave.

"He says that mankind is struggling to classify and study those shadows... and what you have found is that the easiest way to do it is the mathematical one.

"He tells you that you were lucky. Reality could have thrown shadows on the walls of your cave which could have been meaningless, beyond interpretation. He says that your earth is so 'infinitessimal', set against the cosmos, so far out on a minor galactic limb, that the shadows could have been so far from your life on earth as to have made no sense to you at all.

"But your scientists can make sense of what they see - and they see likenesses with life on earth. That's thanks to the nature of the reality outside the cave, which seems to be a mathematical one - pure mathematics, which scientists have plucked from their own inner minds.

"Jeans goes on to say that when the scientists on your planet try to unravel what is shrouded behind the shadows, they come up against your philosopher, Locke, who wrote that 'the real essence of substances' can never be known.

"Jeans reminds you that the philosopher Kant said that man has different ways of seeing nature, but he usually comes back to seeing it through mathematical spectacles.

"Jeans remarks that your primitive ancestors tried to understand nature and in their superstitions they did not prosper. More recent ancestors tried to understand nature as a piece of engineering. What did work spectacularly well were mathematics.

"But the mathematics of the universe, he tells you, do not come from below, from the mathematics of man as Kant supposed. They come from 'above'.

"And indeed Jeans is right. They come from the Holy Ghost, the very Lord of all the dimensions.

"Jeans seems to have realised this. He remarks that Plutarch records that Plato taught that God eternally geometrises. Jeans then comments that obviously Plato meant something else altogether than when you might say 'the banker forever arithmetises.' Plato was almost certainly speaking of the mathematics in the mind of the Most High, The Holy Ghost, creating in the worlds.

"Jeans says that the 'terrestrial pure mathematician' isn't worried about hard matter but about pure thought. He creates thoughts as an engineer creates engines. He says that your understanding of the world is now reduced to pure thought - your ideas of finite space, of space the void, of four, seven and more dimensional space, of space expanding in an expanding universe... of a universe not of cause and effect, but of probability-"

"Probability?" exclaimed Anne incredulously.

"As in a roulette wheel in a casino."

Anne nodded.

"Jeans gave another example of pure thought – happenings which you can account for only by stepping outside of space and time.

"Humourously, Jeans tells you that if space has a boundary and you go outside, the critics complain that all you can find is more space *ad infinitum*. Critics say that proves space cannot be finite; they go on to complain that if the universe is expanding, what is it expanding into if not more space yet?

"Jeans tells you that if you make these criticisms, you are in the mind-set of nineteenth century scientists, who clung to the belief that space could be comprehended physically.

"He says modern science looks at space as a mental construct. Beware, he says, electrons and atoms do not move like the parts of a steam engine. Rather, they dance in a cotillion.

"Jeans argues that the 'true essence of substances' can never be known; then he finds the universe is best portrayed - using poor and inadequate words - as the pure thought of a mathematical thinker."

The white mind-mist said, "And in that, he hit upon the truth - the mathematical thinker is the Most High God, dimly revealing Himself to the denizens of this universe.

"Jeans says the heart of the problem for him is this: atomic activity in a far sun makes it give off heat and light, which travel through the 'ether' as he called it, for nine minutes, to impinge upon our eyeballs, changing the retina, and the disturbance runs along the optic nerve to the brain, which reacts, producing a sensation in the mind, and triggering language... and thus we have poetic musings about the sunset.

"How can an upset among atoms give us poetic thoughts, he asks? The two things are utterly different.

"So Jeans turns to Descartes, and reminds us that Descartes said there could be no joining of mind and matter, two utterly different entities - matter extending in space; and thoughts in the mind. He insisted they were two different worlds.

"Jeans goes on to say that Berkeley and the Idealists agreed with Descartes that if mind and matter were distinct in essence, they could never work on each other.

"But Berkeley and the Idealists said they *do* work on each other; therefore mind and matter must be of the same stuff.

"From there, Berkeley assumed an Eternal Being in whose mind all objects abode and drew life.

"Jeans says, 'Modern science seems to me to lead…' along another road to a conclusion remarkably similar."

The four from Earth sat thoughtfully.

Bo said, "I'm thirsty," and goblets of water materialised beside them.

After they had drunk, the orange light said, "In 500 BC, Pythagoras said the cosmos enjoyed a mathematical order, and that man could understand the universe through numbers. When this was joined to Galileo, Kepler and Francis Bacon, your modern science came into being."

The blue cloud said, "What your mystics found, they found it slipped into their bare minds without space telescopes, cyclotrons, and the rest. And in the West on your planet, let it be said that what were originally naked apes came to invent your machines."

The yellow cloud said, "Your Wolfgang Pauli, of the quantum theory, told you that the only view he could accept was one accepting both sides of reality - measurement and values – the physical and the psychical - accepting at the same time the compatability of them both."

The white cloud said, "Erwin Schrödinger was born on your world in 1887 and died in 1961. He discovered 'wave mechanics' within the theory of the quantum, and 'Schrödinger's wave equation' is the heart of your quantum mechanics.

"Schrödinger was meditating on reality, not simply on science. He said his body worked as a machine following the laws of nature.

"But he said, he knew beyond any argument that it was he who was telling this machine what to do, and foreseeing what might happen. That is, his 'I', his broadest conscious 'I', was controlling atoms.

"Schrödinger says that surely the derivations of that are as near as you can get to proving God and immortality at one blow.

"He recognises that his insight is not the first. To the best of his knowledge, some 2500 years ago the Upanishads considered that Atman equaled Brahman - that the self equaled the ineffable eternal self. For them, this was the quintessential insight into our world.

"Schrödinger muses that you never experience consciousness in the plural... only you alone do. Where you find cases of split personalities, both aren't conscious at once, he says.

"He reflects that consciousness is tightly interwoven with a finite volume of matter, and depends upon it - the body. That, as consciousness is solitary without a plurality, then the plural in the world is perhaps an illusion as you get with a gallery of mirrors - the plural is but different forms of the one.

"He goes on to reflect that for each of us, beyond any argument, all our memories form a one, utterly apart from another person. It is 'I'. But *what is this 'I'?* he demands.

"Look at it closely, he argues, and you find it is rather more than the canvas upon which you painted your memories. He asks, can you not go to a faraway country, never see your friends, practically forget them as you get new friends - and you share life with those new friends as fully as you did with your old. Suppose a hypnotist managed to block all your old memories, your YOU lives on, very much alive. No personal existence is killed.

"'Nor will our existence ever die', he concludes."

Fred said stubbornly, "But we have no direct proof of God's hand in evolution, which is our field."

The green cloud said, "The alphabet of your DNA is G C A and U, you agree? These four nucleotide bricks – or letters – form three-letter words, you call *codons*.

"The three-letter codons go into the *ribosome* to code each for one of the twenty amino-acids. A string of amino-acids comes out the other end of the ribosome, to form different molecules. You agree?

"Now the first two letters join with great reliability.

"The third letter can easily go wrong.

"What did God do?

"Take the amino-acid Proline. The first two letters are CC. So God added all four letters to avoid any mistake.

CCG Proline

CCC Proline

CCA Proline

CCU Proline

"Are you going to tell me that blind nature did that? How did blind nature change the inside of the ribosome so that it would accept not only CCC for Proline, but CCG, CCA and CCU as well? What does the ribosome know of amino-acids? What do the amino-acids know of the ribosome? What do amino-acids and ribosomes know of molecules? WHAT! What indeed.

"Let us look at Leucine, another amino-acid. Here are the codons:

CUG Leucine

CUC Leucine

CUA Leucine

CUU Leucine

"God has taken this trouble to make the transcription fail-safe. Any error can be made in the third letter.

CAG Arginine

CAC Arginine

CAA Arginine

CAU Arginine

"What a loving labour has the Holy Ghost wrought on your world.

ACG Threonine

ACC Threonine

> ACA Threonine
>
> ACU Threonine
>
> AUG Isoleucine
>
> AUC Isoleucine
>
> AUA Isoleucine
>
> AUU Isoleucine…"

Fred shook his head and gave a huge yawn.

Small wine glasses materialised for each person.

The white mind-mist said, "This is a delicious liqueur. Please be our guests."

It was delicious beyond anything they had ever tried, and they all felt a wave of flooding energy, their minds sharpened.

The green cloud went on. "Look at the amino-acid Alanine.

> GCG Alanine
>
> GCC Alanine
>
> GCA Alanine
>
> GCU Alanine

"Shall I give you Serine?

> UCG Serine
>
> UCC Serine
>
> UCA Serine
>
> UCU Serine

"Or Valine?

> GUG Valine
>
> GUC Valine
>
> GUA Valine
>
> GUU Valine

"With this care by the Holy Spirit, how can you get natural evolution, which means beneficial accidents? How many accidents will happen? Almost none, and when they do, the result is usually miscarriage and death. For a creature to evolve into a new form, tens of millions of changes in hundreds of breeding pairs must happen at once - and each change *exact*.

"Let us take a simple change - the sickle cell in the blood that protected Africans from malaria. God changed the 'water-loving' glutamate GAG to the 'water-hating' valine GUG (valine could also be GUC, GUA or GUU, it makes no difference)... He did this on *one exact spot* on the long beta chain for haemoglobin. The water-hating points on the blood molecule are drawn to each other, making a rigid sickle shape. There are a score of amino-acids before and after - had the valine been put somewhere else, it would not have worked. Only the finger of God could do it."

The reddish cloud said, "Einstein has told you that space without matter in it is a void, is no longer space. Buddha said the same - that space without planets or stars was no more space, but nothingness.

"The Holy Spirit created space from nothingness, from non-existence."

The mauve cloud said, "Awesome is the Lord our God, All Mighty, Infinite in Wisdom and Intelligence."

Nicole asked awkwardly, "Are you in direct contact with the Holy Spirit?"

"We are all mystics, and the union of a mystic with God is inexpressible. But God also talks to some spirits through revelation, through images and words that are comprehensible, intelligible," said the beige mind-mist.

The beige cloud went on. "The mystic vision is a seeing, a knowing for our highest understanding, but our middle and lower levels are blind to it. It is full of bliss, ineffable, supernal, a knowing that is yet unknowing. It is a union with the essence that is God, from everlasting to everlasting.

"In revelation, we see God as an immense blinding cloud of love, immense as the whole universe. We do not approach his essence. Revelation does not transcend language, our middle eye.

"The mystical experience transcends language. As your ancient Tao Te Ching writes, 'He who knows does not speak. He who speaks does not know.'

"The mystical union is incomprehensible for he who has had it and for he who has not. It is pure knowing and unknowing. It is the boundlessness of the infinite, of the eternal - it is when your indwelling Spirit is caught up into its God. You are beyond time, death..."

"This talk of the amino-acids and their DNA was revealed to you?" ventured Fred, doubtfully.

The mauve cloud said, "It was revealed. When God changed you humans - changed one hominid for another, he changed millions of codons within the living testicles and ova. He is the living Creator of the worlds and of all life."

The silence lengthened.

The reddish cloud said, "Your Werner Heisenberg lived from 1901 to 1976, and invented your matrix quantum mechanics, which was set into a disciplined form with others helping him - Max Born, Paul Dirac and Wolgang Pauli. This last had as brilliant a mind as Einstein.

"Heisenberg formulated the Heisenberg Uncertainty Principle, which tells you that the more you know about one half of quantum world, the less you can know about the other half. This is important for crossing branes - on earth, you have not reached that.

"Heisenberg wrote that when the Second World War ended, and in the early summer of 1952, atomic physicists gathered in Copenhagen. He tells how three of them were sitting in the conservatory that ran from Niels Bohr's home down to the park - three of your planet's giants, Niels Bohr, Wolfgang Pauli and himself.

"They were remembering how they had sat there twenty-five years ago discussing quantum theory. Niels said, 'Not long ago we had a meeting of philosophers here in Copenhagen - mostly positivists…'"

The beige cloud said, "Those positivists largely argued that you humans can trust only your lowest bridge and they pulled your middle, language-bridge to pieces."

The reddish cloud went on, "They had asked Niels to lecture, and Niels said that when he finished, no one asked questions or argued. Niels was appalled - he told Pauli and Heisenberg, sitting there in the conservatory, that anyone who is not shocked on first meeting quantum theory has understood absolutely nothing.

"Heisenberg writes that that evening Wolfgang Pauli and himself went on talking. They strolled along Copenhagen's Langelinie - the lovely harbour boulevard, that begins to the south near the sleek, metal LITTLE MERMAID that sits close to the shore on a rock.

"Heisenberg told Wolfgang that it would be completely silly to close his ears to earlier philosophers because they didn't use exact language."

The blue cloud said, "Heisenberg wasn't happy to limit himself to his lower understanding, that of his senses."

The reddish cloud went on, "Heisenberg told Wolfgang he often had a lot of trouble understanding what they wanted to say, but he used to try to translate into modern language. He said he had no objection to using the old language of the old religions, that religions resorted to parables and images that had in no way exact meanings.

"He said that the religions talk about *values*, and that the positivists protest you can't find meanings in the vague language of parables. He tried mightily to understand them because he thought they talked about 'a crucial reality'.

"Pauli said, 'If you're thinking that way, then you don't really accept that truth means that you can predict accurately. And what is your idea of truth in science?'

"Heisenberg said thoughtfully that if you looked at Ptolemy's astronomy and Newton's laws of planetary motions, each was as good as the other in predicting the movement of the planets.

"But Newton's equations were the better, and Newton really explained the plan of nature behind the planets."

The mauve cloud said, "The plan of the Holy Spirit in the cosmos, the Idea in the Mind of God."

The reddish cloud said, "Heisenberg said what he meant was the same as the symmetry in the fundamental laws of physics - that symmetry is the key in the plan that nature has created. He said, 'Now I'm talking about *plan* and *created*,' so he said language was really failing him."

The mauve cloud said, "It was not. He was beginning to discern the plan in the Mind of the Holy Spirit, discern the creation of The Right Hand of God."

The reddish cloud went on, "Heisenberg said, perhaps

defensively, that that was his idea of scientific truth – in answer to Pauli's question.

"Wolfgang Pauli then said, 'Niels quotes Schiller's *Truth dwells in the deeps.* Is truth anywhere? Is it these deeps that bind the meaning of life and death?'

"Heisenberg tells us that a few hundred meters away a great liner floated by them, ablaze with lights in the blue dusk. He thought it looked 'fabulous'. He wondered about the life-dramas played behind the cabin windows, and then thought of what Wolfgang had said. What was this liner - a mountain of iron with a huge engine and electricity? Was it the embodying out of human will? Of biological urges forcing protein molecules... steel molecules and electrons?

"He asked himself - was it foolish to quest behind the order in the world for a 'consciousness' that had 'proposed' this order? Was 'consciousness' purely human-centred thinking – should 'consciousness' be confined to the human world? Was there not animal consciousness too?

"'Do we not sense that 'consciousness' expands outside the human order?' he thought.

"These two giants of your planet's science walked on to the northern point of the Langelinie, and then along the jetty. Bright red lay along the horizon - at that latitude the sun barely dips below it at night.

"Pauli asked him suddenly, 'Do you believe in a personal

God? That's a very imprecise question to ask, but you must gather my general idea.'

"Heisenberg said, 'Could I turn your question around? Can we seize the central core of what happens - the core beyond debate - seize it as you would seize upon the soul of another person... stretch out to the soul of that person? I'd reply - yes.'

"Pauli said, 'Then you believe we can know the very core of order as intensely as we can another human's soul?'

"'It's a possibility.'

"'Why do you use the word 'soul'?'"

The blue cloud said, "Here we see a confusion between *soul* and the Inner Spirit living within each person, given straight from the hand of God. On your earth, *soul* is often confused with the middle level, while the Inner Spirit is your higher level alone. When you humans say *soul*, no one can be ever sure about what exactly you are saying."

The reddish cloud resumed, "Heisenberg told him, '*Soul* shows us the exact central core of organisation in the universe, to the inmost heart of a being-'"

The blue cloud interrupted, "He should have said, 'the inmost part of *The Being*-'"

The reddish cloud said, "'... to the inmost heart of a being whose outward manifestations are too multifarious for us to ever understand.'

"The hour was very late, but a ferry tied up to the jetty, to take them back to Kongens Nytertv. From there, they walked back to Neils' place."

The green cloud said, "Your Max Planck told you that the bedrock of all your knowing is grounded in your personal experience. Which is what Heisenberg said - he told you that all science comes from your own experience, and what others tell you of theirs."

The yellow cloud said, "Here we see this fascination with your lower perception - that of the senses. But they are also warning you not to trust that lower level too much."

The beige cloud said, "Consider Robert Oppenheimer, father of the nuclear weapon. He warns you that, 'When we ask whether the electron stays in the same place, we must answer NO. If we ask whether the electron goes somewhere else, we must answer NO. If we ask whether the electron is at rest or is moving, both times we must answer NO'"

The white cloud said, "Here is the beginning of wisdom. But see how your passions subjected your middle intelligence to build atomic bombs. You are not in control of your brains, however often your middle perception glimpses wisdom."

The orange cloud said, "Your Buddha said, 'Transcendental wisdom comes when the reasoning mind reaches its limit; if you are to know the true essence of the world, your thinking has to give way to a higher level of awareness.'"

The white cloud said, "Your Sir Arthur Eddington lived from

1882 to 1944, on your planet. He was a theoretical scientist and thinker.

"He told mankind - suppose we want to defend the mystic. First, we have to admit that physics is but a part only of reality.

"So what then do we do about the other part? It worries us as much as the physical side. Our consciousness is made up of intentions, values, feelings, as much as what our senses tell us."

The orange cloud said, "A human's lower and middle perceptions."

The white cloud went on, "He tells you that your senses lead you to the outside world, the realm of science. But other levels lead you not into space and time but somewhere else.

"'Are we going to suppose that our consciousness,' he says, 'is a waltz of electrons in our brain, and each emotion is a distinct caper; then every bit of consciousness will escort us back into space and time of physics.

"'Would you join me in wondering whether our consciousness goes beyond what we can *measure* in science? Have we got a side of us that *can't be measured*, that doesn't reach out to pet and fondle space and time.

"'We know that our notion of the family table is a self-deception.'"

The four humans looked at each other, and shrugged.

The beige cloud said, "In early writings, Eddington had

pointed out that when you sit at the family table, you think it is hard and solid, of wood, brown in colour... when it is no more than an electro-magnetic haze."

The white cloud said, "He told you that to reach the truth about your family table, you would need other sense organs to braid a new image of it. He said that if your lower levels can build images, what can your higher vision do stepping into a spiritual dimension? The mystic lives as much in that world as he lives on the lower sense world.

"He asks what a mystic would say if we charged him in a scientific court. Surely he would say, 'our day-to-day-world is good enough to get by in, lacking scientific approval, sanction, as it does. I, too, am a tangle of mental delusion in that world, a world my senses probe about in.

"'But I'm far more than my senses. I live in a spiritual world where scientific measurements aren't allowed. Scientific materialism lusts to explain the spirit in a way that will satisfy our lower and middle perceptions.' My words, of course.

"That is why the word *reality* plagues non-believers, because *reality* seems to be much more about religion. Religion handles *reality* as something of momentous gravity, Eddington says, and then asks, how can such a study be profitable?

"He tells you how Dr. Johnson, getting exasperated over an argument on 'Bishop Berkeley's ingenious sophistry to prove the non-existence of matter, and that everything in the universe is merely ideal (he did) strike his foot with mighty force against a large stone, till he rebounded from it, and said, "I refute it thus".'"

The blue cloud said, "I suspect our four guests will find that exhibition as reassuring as I am sure the good Doctor Johnson did."

The white cloud said, "On your planet, the materialist scientists, I fear, would like to measure the kickability quotient of what they are studying and be done with it, but as Eddington tells you, what Rutherford has left of the large stone no longer merits the effort of kicking.

"Eddington goes on to say that many people know that there are realms of human higher consciousness that the world of physics cannot touch. He says you are all born with a yearning, vying towards an Inner Light given from a power mightier than ourselves. Whether in scientific searching or mystical searchings of the spirit, the Light calls.

"He says that 'religion arises from levels of knowing in consciousness that have as much meaning as our sensations. And we have badly mistaken our sensations in analysing the physical world, and science has the job of straightening us out, showing us that things are not what they seem.

"'But we don't gouge out our eyes because they unrepentantly delude us with glorious colours instead of showing us the unvarnished facts of wavelength. We go on living in the middle of this misrepresentation.

"'If the spiritual world has been transformed into something beyond our understanding, that is no reason not to penetrate the misrepresentation we live in to go on to the divine essence in man.'

"They are not his exact words, but that is his meaning. I am putting words into his mouth, paraphrasing him."

Nicole said, "He must have said that decades ago, and a thousand light years away. No problem."

The white mind-mist said, "Eddington goes on to say he's giving no proofs. He says the mathematician abases himself before *proof*, but in physics they have another idol - *plausibility*. In science, he often feels that the answer given is believable – and equally that he can feel from a spiritual sphere that religious belief can be right. He says that you create your spiritual world from your personalities as you fashion your scientific world from the measurements of your mathematicians.

"He remarks that the sublimity felt from the spirit gets easily lost in the mean and grievous everyday life on your planet. He urges you towards spirit-to-spirit rapport with the World Spirit despite your burdens and obligations.

"'Will people think I've been jawing well-intentioned absurdities?' he asks, 'Physical science has sturdy balustrades to keep us out of the swamps. But balustrades or not, we can't proceed from electrons and the rest of physics to explain a man's consciousness.

"'Some people talk about a human mechanism knee-jerking to the world by reflexes, but that won't hold good for the moral or religious man. Those days when a vain-glorious and conceited physics wouldn't let a man call his soul his own have passed.'

"He mentions *Alice Through the Looking Glass*, that relativistic, quantum fable. The relativistic Red Queen states forcibly, 'You call that nonsense, but I've heard nonsense compared with which that would be sensible in a dictionary.'

"He says that his brain can multiply 7 by 8 and produce 56, while churning out sugar... it has behaved impeccably, following the laws of physics. But whatever it churns up by the laws of physics, a physical mechanism can't value or desire something.

"However, he says that on your planet in your year of 1927 religion at last became accessible for the scientific man... that, and most ordinary life too, such as falling in love. In 1927, cause and effect were swept off the board by Heisenberg, Bohr, Born and others. The world is a roulette wheel.

"Can you humans now step back from your fight between science and religion? Eddington says you can if you will but respect the frontier in between. On one side of the frontier, theologians state that a future, non-material life awaits you in heaven. On the other side, the scientist states that space and time are a continuum, and the notion of heaven in future time is more upsetting to him than the idea held before Copernicus that it was in space, up above your heads.

"Who is right? That is not the question to ask.

"The question to ask is whether someone has jumped across the frontier and invaded the lands of the other. Let theology treat of the human soul in a non-material realm; and let science treat of the geometry of space-time.

"Eddington says, 'I think the notion of a universal Mind or Logos would be a reasonably correct deduction from today's science. An inner sense of what is right guides us in science, and we have an inner thread that leads us to a spiritual world.

"'It is true that our senses grossly betray us in the world we inhabit, and perhaps our consciousness may lead us astray when we try to step into the spiritual world. That doesn't mean we can't try.

"'Let the scientific materialist who believes all he sees and feels comes from electrons and quanta obeying mathematical laws; let him also accept that his wife is a labored differential equation. If this scientific rigidity might lead to an obdurate domestic response, it is surely inappropriate for the human soul approaching the divine spirit.' Or some such words.

"He goes on, 'See me standing in a doorway. Frightening business. I have to push against an air pressure of fourteen pounds a square inch all over my body. I have to put my foot squarely upon a board travelling at 20 miles a second around the sun. If I get it wrong, the board could be miles away. I hang from a round planet with my head sticking out into space.

"'The board isn't solid, but like a swarm of flies.'

"He means, an electromagnetic field, a haze. The flies are knots, huge concentrations of energy that give us particles in our universe.

"He says, 'Will my foot plunge through the swarm? Will I fall?

"'Verily, it is easier for a camel to pass through the eye of needle than for a scientist to get through a door.

"'Especially a church door.'"

After a silence, the white cloud said, "So you humans grope this way and that on your planet."

After another silence, the beige mind-mist said, "Sir Arthur Eddington also said that the down-to-earth scientists find it hard to think of everything as being mental, but mind is your first and only experience; you only infer the rest."

The blue cloud said, "Talking about atoms, 'we must use poetry, poetic language', Niels Bohr said."

The orange cloud said, "He also said that the idea of a world out there that was physically independent – that no longer holds, neither for the world of matter itself, nor for the observer."

The yellow cloud said, "Sir Arthur Eddington said that the world of matter is an abstraction, an idea without reality except where it touches human consciousness."

The reddish cloud said, "John Wheeler said that four-dimensional space-time is but a mental construct."

The green cloud said, "Erwin Schrödinger said that the infinite variety humans see in the world is but an illusion; it isn't real."

The beige cloud said, "We come back to Sir Arthur Eddington, who said that the outside world of human physics has turned into a world of penumbra. Taking away your delusions, scientists took away the substance, because you have had to see that substance, hard matter, is one of the worst of your delusions."

The yellow cloud said, "Max Planck wrote that it is impossible for you to know the world through your senses and intelligence. It's a world beyond your mental powers."

The whitish cloud said, "Prince Louis de Broglie lived on your planet from 1892 until 1987. As a student in 1923, he presented two papers on 'matter waves', which later went into his doctoral thesis. They sent the thesis to Einstein, who gave wide circulation to his ideas, and from this thesis Erwin Schrödinger developed the Schrödinger wave equations. In 1929, de Broglie had the Nobel Prize in Physics.

"De Broglie tells us that in the last chapter of his MORALITY AND RELIGION, the French philosopher Henri Bergson showed mankind reeling under the mechanisms of its discoveries. Bergson wrote how petrol, coal and hydro-electricity now drive machines, burning energies gathered over millions of years, and gave your puny species immense powers out of all proportion to your size. He said the spirit now was too small to fill such an immensely enlarged frame.

"De Broglie takes exception, and declares that your overgrown body awaits the fulfillment of a soul - the machines demand mystics.

"He warns that the atomic bomb gives even newer powers to man, powers hidden at the heart of nature. Will atomic energy bring a higher and nobler life?

"He cries a warning. Human passions don't change, and the nightmare of the Second World War made the whole earth run with blood.

"While man's control of his world was bounded, the consequences of what he did were restrained. Modern wars throw greater hosts of soldiers into the holocaust, open civilians to the same dangers as an armed soldier. Fifty years ago, he writes, anarchists shocked the world by throwing bombs into public places and killing a few people; today's bombs raze whole cities.

"He calls upon the guides of humanity! Those who have the mission of leading humanity to spirituality must awaken humanity to its soul... before it is too late."

The blue cloud said, "Einstein tried to tell humans that they were born to serve, not to rule.

"How true! When the will of one single man on earth can destroy and kill!

"Einstein went further. He urged you humans to live harmonious lives, abandoning materialistic wishes. Did not Einstein say, to truly judge someone, ask how liberated is he from his self.

"In another profound saying, he said that nothing teaches and purifies like failure and having to do without.

"You humans hate doing without. But Sir James Jeans told you that the best way to understand the universe is to understand that it is made of pure thought."

Fred said, "But you can't eat pure thought. *I* see."

The eight beings turned towards him in a silence that lasted minutes.

The mauve cloud said, "Reality rises up from a deep order which closes it back in. Then it opens up. It opens and closes."

After a long silence, Fred said, "I don't understand."

The green cloud said, "Max Planck told you to look for the elementary thing from which the secondary thing has flowed; look for the absolute behind what passes; for the reality behind what you seem to see; for what lasts behind what comes and goes; in physics and in life."

Fred shook his head.

The yellow cloud said, "Einstein told you that you live in 'chaotic diversity'. Science tries to make theories to bring order to things, to your senses, to the lower perceptions of your senses. But all theories are fabrications by men. There is no certainty in the world as you see it."

Bo held out his hands helplessly. He said, "I'm like Dr, Johnson. If I kick a big rock, it hurts, I bruise, and I don't like pain: you can't argue with pain."

The reddish cloud said, "Werner Heisenberg said that you

divide the world in seer and seen, subject and object, body and soul. 'That doesn't work any more, and gets us into every sort of difficulty!' he cries."

Nicole said, "I don't see any difficulty. I'm me, and a chair is a chair. We're completely separate."

The whitish cloud said, "You are and you are not, and to understand that is the beginning of wisdom. On one side is your indwelling immortal Spirit. On the other side is your brain, the chair, your body, the rocks on the ground. To divide your self and your not-self is untrue; the division is between your self and not self on the one side, and your Self given from God on the other. Yet they can join, because all is of God."

The white cloud said, "Sir Arthur Eddington tried to tell you that the stuff of your experience is mind-stuff. He says that doesn't quite mean *mind* and *stuff*, because he's speaking broadly. By mind-stuff he means something beyond your personal consciousness... and yet something not altogether alien to your consciousness.

"He says that your imagination has woven the ideas of matter and fields of force, although they have about as much to do with underlying reality as a bursar's accounts have to do with what goes on in a university.

"He recognises that we have self-knowledge of our mental activity in the world - no surprise there – and this 'mind' is not in space and time.

"Everything that you know of the outside world - and from

this comes your physics - has been coded and transmitted along your nerves to your consciousness. When you code for the family table, the code has not the faintest likeness to the table itself that sent off the message, nor to the image of the table that comes into being inside your consciousness.

"The neurons in your brain are part of your mental world, but psychology cannot analyse neurons.

"Nor, he says, can you equate your middle mind with your higher consciousness. Your middle mind can hold unconscious, repressed memories that are not in your consciousness. Your consciousness descends towards your subconscious, and there your consciousness withers away. He asks, is not self-awareness of consciousness something that escapes scientific explanation?

"He believes you have but one angle of attack - through direct awareness of your three levels. He laments that many scientists are unhappy indeed that underlying everything - including pain after kicking a big stone - is mental. He sees in the standoff between the material and spiritual world a parallel in the tenseness between science and religion.

"He says that your higher, third level ever beckons you; that you get twitchy contemplating a world without God. Unreadable are the ways of God, but within you persists that religious feeling that God should show His power through miracles and signs, reassure you that the universe lies under His Hand.

"No scientist will confess to feeling the lack of an inscrutable, omnipotent Spirit to guide the atoms and the stars - a Spirit who our consciousness divines as there. And if the scientist did, Eddington fears, he would try to wrap up God in differential equations - differential equations being that unfailing recourse for scientists to restore order in the universe.

"Differential equations belong to the scientific world of measurements, he reminds us, and not to the laws of the spiritual ground of being."

The four from earth sat in silence. Then Anne said, "This idea of two realities - okay. But you equate us with rocks on the one hand, with Spirit on the other."

The beige cloud, "As God is creator, the two can join under God."

"The mind of God holds infinite mathematical orders, statements, equations - some simple and some of infinite complexity.

"The physical realm is His 'materialisation of thought' as someone said on your planet, the materialisation of *His* thought. Matter is a densifying, an irruption of His mind, of his mathematics, into physical space, obeying His mathematical laws - but only a small number of His mathematical statements and equations.

"With rocks, His mathematics are simpler; with mankind they are intricate. A single cell in your bodies is of such complexity that perhaps your brains will never come to understand it. Each cell lives in a 'sea', the cytoplasm, and to communicate, rather than thrust molecules out of the cell into the sea, where they could be carried away, cells are joined by micro-tubes to safely exchange cellular contents - a tangled mathematics from the mind of God as to defy your understanding completely.

"Einstein told you that, in the universe *you know*, and *understand*, 'Nature springs from conceivable mathematical forms.' Because where the Lord's mathematics are inconceivable for you, there you cannot understand the universe.

"Be that as it may, matter is an abstracted translation of God's Idea.

"As your Plato said, matter is a shadow on the wall of your cave. What your scientists do is to seek, with their second-level sight, what mathematics have fleshed out into this physcial universe within this dimension, and then check with their lowest sight - their senses."

The yellow cloud said, "Your sages over thousands of years have told you of this, without knowing science. An ancient Buddhist said that space and time are but names.

"Another sage said that humans easily fit names to understand the world, but then treat the names as though they were real.

"An ancient Chinese sage told you that weigh what a man knows and it is nothing compared to the weight of his ignorance.

"Another told you that subject and object are two sides of the same consciousness."

The blue cloud said, "On your planet, it has been written

for more than two thousand years that the mind of God is a great ocean, its surface rough with waves and tides, its depth Unmoved.

"Another saying told you that the outside world arises only from the mind itself - you think it is outside of you because you cannot reason truly.

"Another sage warned you that reality is One - unchanging, without form, infinite and eternal. Why would you divide it? There is no seer, nor seeing, nor seen."

The green cloud said, "Is it not written on your planet that has He not created ten thousand ages but dwells in Oneness."

The mauve cloud said, "Einstein told you that no one can distinguish between mass and energy. Energy has mass and mass has energy. He told you to think of matter as a place where the energy is immensely strong.

"Heisenberg told you that the elementary particles are not of matter; they are energy which has taken on the shape of an elementary particle. The same for an atom. An atom is not a 'thing'.

"Sir James Jeans told you that you live on the surface of a deep river. Bubbles and eddies form on the surface, coming from below. These are energy and radiation which create matter.

"A particle is just a minute domain of the energy field where the field concentrates immense power - a mighty field-energy knot and you have an electron - the knot moves through space like a wave. It can be anywhere on the wave of its probable locations. A ripple on the ocean of energy.

"As Buddha said, the knowing person wipes away all 'things'.

"These particles are not indestructible, as Heisenberg told you. They can change into one another.

"Here there is no cause and effect. As Neils Bohr warned you, when you think you see cause and effect, it is to make yourselves feel more comfortable."

The beige cloud said, "Sir James Jeans told you that you cannot reach into the 'real essence of substances', and so that blotches the line between realism and thought. Large stones, and tigers in thickets, exist because your lower perceptions all agree; but he says it's a better and safer call to solve the disagreement with mathematics.

"He asks you what is *substantiality*? No more than a mental measurement of the effect of teeth, rocks, door handles and the bodywork of cars on your lower sense of touch... but they are better to be thought of as hosts of hard energy knots, particles, without calling them more or less substantial. Science progresses, but Dr. Johnson goes on 'dashing his foot against a stone.'

"You have no outside tape-measure to measure substantiality with, only your own lower sense of touch, but you can agree that things can be of a different degree.

"He says, however, that the idea of the cosmos as one of pure thought gives a new line of attack."

Fred said, "I can't understand this talk of One Mind, pure thought in the universe."

The other three nodded. Nicole said, "Our consciousness is fixed inside our head, and must have something to do with our brains."

The blue cloud said, "The brain holds trillions of synapses between neurons. When you are angry, IS your consciousness angry, or does it FEEL angry?"

Nicole said, "I FEEL angry, although in a rage I know some people lose all sense of their consciousness. Rage overwhelms them."

The blue cloud said, "Your consciousness gets input from the brain - your dictionaries back on your planet list some two thousand words for emotions. Your psychologists number about five thousand possible personality traits and types of person.

"These all assail your consciousness, but your consciousness goes on, unyielding, no matter what the violent feelings. In one man's life, his overpowering tone can be depressive - another, usually optimistic. This coloring arises from the brain, which your consciousness FEELS.

"Can you see this independence? Can you conceive of a divine Consciousness covering the cosmos?"

Anne shook her head. "If I feel frightened, I feel frightened!"

"Is your 'I' frightened, or does it FEEL frightened?"

"Everything's frightened inside me!"

"Your thinking is confused."

"I can't see it, see the confusion."

Bo said, "It's hard to say."

Fred said, "I don't know what to think."

Nicole said, "It could be as you say - I don't know what to think either."

After some minutes, the beige cloud said, "Coming back to Sir James Jeans - he says that energy is the fundament of the universe, and is best handled by mathematics. He says that mathematical formulae never tell you what a thing is exactly, but they do tell you what it does. Modern science can only pinpoint a thing through its traits, not say what it is.

"He says that if the cosmos is indeed a cosmos of thought, then an act of thought created it. He insists that the closed limits of time and space constrain him to see the creation as a thought. The diameter of the universe, the number of elementary particles; these are numbers that overwhelmingly suggest thought.

"On top of that, modern scientific theory forces you to think of a creator working outside of his creation, as a painter stands apart from his canvas. He quotes your St. Augustine: *Non in tempore, sed cum tempore, finxit Deus mundum.* 'Not inside time, but with time, did God create the world.'

"Even your Plato says that 'Time and the firmament were born at the same moment... Such was the thought in the mind of God when He created time.'

"Jeans insists that scientists generally, today, almost all of them, think alike... that the universe is looking more and more like a mighty thought than a mighty machine."

The four from earth looked puzzled.

"He says that what you have found is that the universe is not inimical to life but that substantial hard matter dissolves into a creation and a flowering of mind. You have found a designer, a mathematician. You have found that thought shaped those first inert atoms in the primeval slime.

"Yet you four paleontologists would tell us that those dead atoms gathered themselves together intelligently or by some prodigious accident, and evolved LIFE!"

The four from the earth didn't answer.

Fred said, "Didn't Jeans always say that he was always supposing - speculating?"

The beige cloud said, "Indeed he did. But we eight can tell you that his guesses were inspired."

Small goblets appeared before the four from earth, with the

aromatic liqueur. They seized them, and sipped, avidly; then sat up straighter, their eyes quickened.

The white mind mist said, "Heisenberg also talks to you about the Greeks; Plato and Democritus. He was in Greece, and dreams how, on the Aegean coast, millennia ago, Leucippus and Democritus struggled with the make-up of matter; while down in the market-place Socrates argued about your use of words, and Plato taught that the Idea stood behind all the manifestations which met your eyes.

"Heisenberg mused that two thousand five hundred years had passed, and men's minds had toiled without rest over these unknowns. He said that today he had a huge advantage - the new findings in atomic physics.

"But things were not that easy... Leucippus and Democritus had worked out a philosophy of materialism, over which battles have raged since modern science came on the scene in the sixteen hundreds. Dialectical materialism has steamrollered politics in the nineteenth and twentieth centuries.

"The role that ideas about matter have played in European society! An explosive role. But the new findings have turned human life upside down, all over the world, he reflected.

"He asked himself, how does modern experimental physics compare with the ancient philosophy of Greece...? He felt that modern atomic theory shows Plato to have been closer to the truth than Leucippus and Democritus.

"Heisenberg remembered how in the first days in ancient

Greece, they disputed over the *one* and the *many*. An ever-changing, bewildering variety of things overwhelm your senses; the Greeks wanted to track them back to one fount.

"Leucippus and Democritus argued for the atom. For them, it was indestructible, eternal, the only truly existing object in the universe; all other things existed only thanks to the atom, as their appearances came and went, and changed.

"They argued that between the atoms lay the void, and that empty space left room for them to move. But in themselves, there was no change, only pure existence.

"The arguments of Leucippus and Democratus allowed for water, steam and ice - the atoms could move loosely, not too close together; or could be widely apart; or could be densely clinging in ice. 'In our day, these ideas were to be very productive.'

"But in your day, they were to prove a stumbling block. You think of the atom as a bit of something, a brick to build with. Its state of pure being yields to thoughts about its characteristics, its placing and how it moves. The atoms can even stretch a little in space - which is the end of the idea that they are indivisible. If the atom is spatial, why can't you divide it?

"But the Greeks did put you on the right track. All that you see in rocks, trees, steel beams and cars — you can bring it all down to the placing and the moving of atoms.

"But now the headache. *What* decides where the atoms will go and how they will move? The Greeks balked at answering that, says Heisenberg. They did not have your ideas of natural laws, but, certainly, they did talk of cause and effect.

"The whole idea of the Greeks was to see beyond the 'many' to the 'one'- the atom - which explained all the forms. This was not going to work without your modern idea of natural laws to explain away changes in place and speeds of this atom of theirs.

"The Greek philosophers did argue about natural laws, but they saw them as fixed and frozen, a geometry in space. They saw the round orbits of the planets, and regular geometrical shapes, and thought they were lasting constructions in the natural world.

"When Plato came into the fray against Leucippus and Democritus, he assented to their smallest bits of matter, but took heated exception to the philosophy of supposing all existence rested upon them... that they were the only true corporeal bodies.

"No, Plato's atoms were less than material, Heisenberg tells you. They were geometrical shapes, the stuff of mathematicians. These bits in some way were of, or emanated from, the Ideas that were the ground of the solid universe, and moved matter this way and that.

"Speaking rigorously, Heisenberg writes, for Plato they weren't really atoms, not indivisible bits. Plato thought triangles had formed them, and by an exchange of triangles, you could change matter. As triangles are 2-D, they weren't corporeal – not hard matter. When you reached the end of possible divisions, the smallest bit was a mathematical shape. This shape decides how the smaller bits of matter will acquit themselves - and from that, what matter itself will do.

"This came into the very essence of Plato's idealist philosophy. Ideas are the ground of objects, of bodies. The smallest bits of matter grow into the visible frame whereby we can see the world: but they were originally mathematical frames.

"From this Platonic philosophy, says Heisenberg, comes today the saying, 'God is a mathematician.'"

"How can He be God and be a mathematician?" grumbled Fred.

The white cloud said, "Your God is Wonderful, Marvellous, your Everlasting Father, Prince of Love, of Inimitable Wisdom, Counsellor, Infinitely Consoling... of Awesome Might and Power, the very Lord of the Universes, of the Dimensions, and of the Earth from whence you have come..."

The four sat speechless.

The reddish cloud said, "Atoms and subatomic particles are in endless cotillion, flicker, ebb and flow, flux, boil, cascade, come into being and vanish - the protons and neutrons in the nucleus whirl around at 44,000 miles a second. Nothing is still, nothing is fixed, is in permanent being - all is racing, changing. Everything depends on the rest; one random mosaic flows into the next. Nothing is sure, only probable.

"To measure, you must make assumptions - that the processes

and fleeting 'particles' are the same whatever way the apparatus faces, or wherever you put it. That the shadowy subatomic 'particles' and processes do not change with the speed that the observer travels at. That if particle 'A' changes to 'B', then 'A' appears before 'B', following the arrow of time as you humans understand the arrow. Energy first knots into 'A', then unknots to knot into 'B'.

"Change those rules, and your universe changes.

"In other words, what you humans see depends on what you suppose when you set up your apparatus.

"So the world you 'see' is your mental creation, and does not reflect God's true reality.

"It reflects the apparatus you choose. And your kicking a stone on your planet depends on your brains and on your nervous systems.

"You see a world where the stone is fixed - that it will change it ten or hundred years does not enter into your immediate mind picture."

Bo said aggressively, "So that stone's not there!"

The orange cloud said, "A sage speaking from his higher level of perception would say it doesn't matter, because there is no matter. Your Beatles sang, 'Let it be, let it be.' He would tell you, 'Let it be.'"

"So the pain from the kick is all in our heads," said Nicole. "Well, that's enough for me. Pain is pain, and is real."

The beige cloud said, "The only reality is that of the Lord, your Almighty and Everlasting God, Ruler of all the Dimensions, who has created the fleeing and ceaseless dance of particles ever dissolving into one another. As your Bible says, here there is no continuing city.

"Does not your Eastern Ashaghosha teach, 'If you don't recognise the oneness of all things, the detailed mind is ignorant... everything that appears in the cosmos is but a deceitful, unsubstantial construct of your mind and is unreal!' I paraphrase him.

"Your ancient Buddhist teachings say that mind throws up images and thoughts without end, and you call them your outside world. None of it is really out there. It is all in your mind only."

The four sat, bereft of words.

After several minutes, Bo squared his shoulders, and asked, "That lifeboat we found inside the mountain - was that yours?"

"No. That is from another planet, another civilisation, some three thousand years ahead of yourselves."

"And you are ahead of them?"

"Our civilisation is about one million years old. We all

belong to the Confederation, and when needed, those people, who brought you here, get more advanced technology from ourselves."

"Have your ships ever landed on earth?"

"About a million years ago. We landed on earth, on Mars, on the moons of Jupiter, on Pluto, doing a full survey.

"We mastered space flight about a million years ago, and soon could travel at three-quarters the speed of light. So we sent ships out in every direction, and after one hundred and twenty five years, more or less, we had explored a sphere up to about one hundred light years out. It took a hundred years for our reports to get back from the most distant ships, but we built up a library.

"After two thousand years, we had information from some seven hundred and fifty light-years away in every direction.

"We found new planets, who showed us life on other planets thousands of light years out."

The silence lengthened.

The white cloud finally spoke. "We were talking about Plato, on your world.

"Heisenberg talks about Plato suggesting that God was a mathematician. He says the sheer significance of this proposition 'can hardly be reckoned too highly'. He says that ushered in mathematical science... and led to defining the word 'understanding'. Of all the ways of understanding in science, science pinpoints mathematical 'truth' as the 'true' understanding.

"From which derives measurements. Most of modern science was based on measurement.

"Heisenberg goes on to say this: from Newton until today, we see physicists putting forward different sets of natural laws. In the twentieth century, he says, we have the new laws of quantum theory governing the outer shells of chemical atoms, and so explaining chemistry. Laws between relativity and quantum theory are still a sticking point.

"Back in your nineteenth century, advances in chemistry and heat stuck closely to what Leucippus and Democritus had said. Materialism revived, and dialectical materialism swept the political world.

"Then you found that chemical atoms were built of smaller parts - electrons, and the nuclei of protons and neutrons. They still looked like materialistic atoms - to the point that you could see a single one in a cloud or bubble chamber. That was one up for Leucippus and Democritus - they looked like corporeal things, the same as rocks or trees do.

"But the headache for you - the materialistic atom - had been nagging the ancient debate too - and now today that is acute. Are the smallest bits really ordinary bits of matter, the way sand and gravel are? Heisenberg said that the coming of the quantum theory decades ago settled that two thousand five hundred year-old argument. He says that our ordinary language, ordinary thinking no longer will do. You cannot describe the position, speed, size and color of atoms the way you can describe cars driving in a city.

"But mathematical language can describe them, with precision. And your high-energy accelerators are showing you more and more about elementary particles.

"Heisenberg asks - who was right?

"Democritus or Plato?

"He says that modern physics has fallen on the side of Plato. As Plato had said, the smallest bits are forms, shapes - or Ideas to use his very word. Ideas that mathematics can define beyond any argument.

"Today, in modern theoretical physics on your planet the job is to draw up the natural law ordering elementary particles.

"As Heisenberg said, 'It was an unbelievable achievement' for the ancient philosophers to have put all the right questions.

"He goes on that the quest for the 'one' final explanation of everything gave birth to religion and science.

"But in the sixteenth and seventeenth centuries, science went up a different path - that of experimentation. This led to the rift, which began with the Church's trial of Galileo. In ancient Greece, Heisenberg reminds you, they put Socrates to death for contradicting their religion.

"The scientists held their obsessive stare on a *materialistic* 'one'. In the nineteenth century, that stare had not wavered. Scientists stood against Christian philosophy.

"Today, in modern atomic science, you use complex, advanced mathematics of sharp clarity. Your scientists have finally seen that they cannot talk about the atomic world in the language of philosophy and theology, but must use mathematics. All they can say in their everyday language, says Heisenberg, is that 'God is a mathematician.'

"Plato had run up against the same barrier. He turned to poetry, to images from deep in the human unconscious, to images that show the hidden form of the world. Heisenberg says that, in language, only images and allegories can approach the 'one'."

A long silence followed.

Then the beige cloud spoke, and said, "Your scientist, Max Planck, another of your giants, was born in 1858 and died in 1947. In 1900, he made a staggering leap and announced that nature was not continuous, but came in packets - in quanta."

The white cloud said, "If nature were continuous, then it would partake of the eternal reality. Nature is but a creation in the Mind of God."

The beige cloud said, "The father of the quantum theory, they gave him the Nobel Prize in 1918.

"He has written to tell you that that you might well suppose that modern science tells you to put the idea of miracles right out of your minds. He says that science *does no such thing*. Because is there a point where cause-and-effect thinking can't go?

"He says there is - there is a single point in the immeasurable world of the brain and of things where science won't work. This is the personal self. In the original German in which Planck wrote, he used the expression for I-ness, I AM-ness, for the unassailable, irrefutable, indivisible Self.

"He says that here abides free will and freedom, and on this higher level of yourselves, 'we can create what we wish.' The enduring, perennial awareness, defying all science, shows the immunity of the Self to the laws of cause and effect. All science can do is bring you to the doorstep of your Self, and there it leaves you to your own devices.

"You live your life free of the iron law of logic - no causes can inflexibly fix your future, no 'today' can tell you infallibly what your future will be.

"Any one single happening can shape your ends as all the wisdom on Earth can never do. So he asks, what is it that does shape our ends when our intellectual gifts hardly can?

"He says that intelligence has to yield to character, and science to religion.

"Which brings him to the vexed struggle between science and religion.

"He says that religion belongs to a world that is unalterable, inflexible before cause-and-effect, that lies beyond science. The experimental world of the scientists rests on cause-and-effect, so no true antagonism obtains.

"He says that every serious man has to see in his nature a religious spirit, which he should nourish, so that all his powers - his lower, middle and higher levels - can harmonise. It's no accident, he says, that the greatest thinkers were deeply religious, whether they made it public or not.

"Science elevates moral values, Planck tells you, because the scientist loves and reverences the truth; he grows in reverence because every discovery brings him closer to the mystery of his being in this world.

"In a conversation, Planck said that churches no longer give the spiritual stability that people need, so people turn elsewhere.

"*Religion demands belief.*

"Science is no substitute for religion, because science also calls for belief. Over the gates of science these words are inscribed: Ye must have faith. You can't just experiment blindly. You must know what you are looking for, and have faith that you will find it. You follow your hypothesis, sprung from your imagination. You have to choose and eliminate as you go forward: if your imaginary plan collapses, you keep the faith and build another plan.

"Look at Kepler, he says. Kepler was always broke, begging for the back payments of his salary from the Reichstag in Regensburg. He had the atrocious torment of defending his own mother against charges of witchcraft.

"But he was untiring, invincible, such was his faith in his own science, his faith in a plan behind creation, a plan behind the astronomical movements.

"Tycho de Brahe had no faith in the divine laws of creation. He had the same means as Kepler, and more money, but was never more than a researcher.

"Science can never solve the deepest mysteries, because we are part and parcel of nature's mystery which we try to solve. Everywhere, we are brought up short by what seems irrational, and only faith keeps us going. Science is the pursuit of the incomprehensible, the known and unknown as seen by our consciousness.

"But science can never replace religion, he tells you."

Fred said sourly, "I understand belief in science..."

A long silence fell.

Anne said, "I never studied physics. Could you tell me more about quantum?"

The yellow cloud said, "The universe shows us mind on three levels," and the four from earth frowned.

The yellow cloud went on, "At the lowest level, we find the elementary physical activities of quantum mechanics. Here, matter in quantum mechanics is constantly choosing, always under probabilistic laws. Every time we experiment, we oblige nature to choose.

"Just as our minds make choices, each electron has a 'mind' that chooses."

Anne looked at him blankly.

"At the middle level, we find mind from our own lives. Our brains seem to be enormous amplifiers of the 'mind' inside the quantum."

The four looked shocked.

"At the higher level, we find a mental entity in the universe as a whole. It is as though the lower and middle levels are small parts of the Primordial Mind, the Primordial creator, that is God."

The orange cloud said, "Suppose you have film showing the Milky Way, and you can *see* the Milky Way on the film. You can project an image of the galaxy.

"If you cut that film in half, then you will project only *one-half* of the Milky Way.

"But suppose on an original hologram film you can't see anything. Use the laser, and you see your 3-D projection.

"Then cut *that* film in half - and with the laser you'll still get the whole Milky Way. Cut it in quarters - cut it in sixteen pieces - in 240 pieces - and each small piece, however tiny, will show you *the entire Milky Way*. In that sort of film - in that hologram - every part holds the whole hologram.

"Plotonius was a bridge between Plato and the Early Christian Fathers. Plotonius wrote, almost two thousand years ago, 'See all things not as evolving but as already in Being, each seeing itself in the other. Each unit of being holds inside itself the whole intelligible world. The All is in each. Each is in the All. And the All *is* each. Man has departed from the All, but when he throws off his individuality, he goes back into the entirety of the World.

"In China, the ancient Book of the Tao, from the fourth and third centuries BC, told you, 'Ask not whether the First is this or that. It is in every being. It has limited each thing, but Itself is without limit, is infinite.'

"The Christian Saint Catherine of Genoa explained it in words that no one can mistake. 'My Me is God, nor do I accept any other Me save my God himself.'

"The Christian Meister Eckhart told you, but do you listen on that planet of yours? 'To measure what the soul holds, we must measure it against what God holds, for the Ground of God and the Ground of your Spirit are the same.'

"You are part of God's hologram.

"Eckhart further says, 'The knower and the known are the same. Simple folk imagine that God stands *there* and that they stand *here*. Not so. God and I are one.

" 'There is no need for goodness and knowledge to enter you. They are inside you already… but you are blind to them.' "

The green cloud said, "You see multiplicity in countless, bewildering forms. All those different things on your planet are but one, all within the oneness of the hologram."

The reddish cloud asked, "Do you read the magazine, SCIENTIFIC AMERICAN?"

All four nodded.

The reddish cloud went on, "Jacob Bekenstein, Polak Professor of Theoretical Physics at the Hebrew University at Jerusalem wrote in that magazine about the hologram. He said that William Blake had written how you could see the universe in a grain of sand. Bekenstein wrote that while a grain of sand might not hold our universe, a flat screen well might."

Nicole gasped, "He wrote about *GOD'S* hologram!"

"No, nothing about God. He showed how it was probably a hologram out there.

"He explained how the American mathematician Claude Shannon in 1948 introduced a way of measuring the amount of information held somewhere – 'entropy'"

The four scowled. Fred said angrily, "Entropy means disorder. It means a vase can fall and break on the floor – but the bits on the floor can't rise to the tabletop and put themselves together again."

Anne said, "You've lost us, I'm sorry."

The yellow cloud said, "Sorry. Let's go back to the beginning. We need to measure how much info there is - all right?"

The four smiled, relieved.

"Back in 1877, the Austrian physicist Ludwig Boltzmann

worked out how to show all the different microscopic mosaics that particles could form in a lump of matter while it went on looking just the same to us. Shannon ended up with equations like Boltzmann's. Shannon said the content of a message depends on how many binary bits you need to codify it. Those bits really have no dimensions, and don't tell us what the message is actually saying.

"What matters for Shannon is the freedom of the bits to arrange themselves - that is, a bit's freedom, in its place and speed. Of course, all a chip cares about is whether the bit is ON or OFF.

"How far can freedom go - can go in God's hologram? Bekenstein reminds the reader that atoms are electrons and nuclei - the nuclei are made of protons and neutrons, and in turn are made of quarks – and on your world, your scientists incline to believe that quarks are made of strings. But, says Bekenstein, there could be more levels than anyone on earth has ever dreamt of."

"Are there more?" demanded Bo.

The whitish-cloud said, "We cannot interfere with your planet. We cannot reveal that to you."

The yellow cloud said, "In a holographic film, you use photons. But Bekenstein asks, suppose we use quarks? How much holographic info could we then fit into a cube of, say, one centimetre? Or if you used strings! He says you could consider the Planck length, about 10^{-33} centimetre, which is the smallest length used in your gravity and quantum mechanics. He is now talking about unimaginable amounts of info packed into the smallest space.

"But, he warns, we are limited by the outside envelope, the boundary, the outside skin of confinement. Volume inside grows much more quickly than the outside skin. You double the hull of a submarine and you get far more than double the volume inside. If you crowd too much info inside, the outside skin doesn't stretch fast enough, so you have to stop. You can't squeeze any more in.

"In 1995, Leonard Susskind at Stanford University determined the holographic bound - how much info can be stuffed into a certain space, into so much matter and energy.

"Bekenstein explains that a holograph one centimetre across could hold 10^{66} bits - when the visible universe holds about 10^{100}. So all the info about our visible universe could be crammed and stowed in a hologram ball about one-tenth of a light-year across."

The beige cloud said, "As you can see only a couple of percent of the universe, you would still need a hologram as big as the universe itself to see it all. But it doesn't matter - all the info is stacked in each small segment, although more hazily. So you can access all God's hologram at any point."

The green cloud said, "Bekenstein asks, 'Does the holographic idea apply to our universe?' He says your universe, as perceived on earth, is 4-D... three dimensions, changing with time. He says that would need a 3-D hologram for 4-D physics.

"But, he says, your scientists and mathematicians are now talking about various dimensions, about a hologram drawn in many dimensions, because then the maths come out right. An intelligent being living in one of these dimensions wouldn't know whether he was living in a 5-D universe of superstrings, or a 4-D one with quantum fields and point particles."

Fred exploded, "He actually believes there is a hologram out there!"

The mauve cloud replied, "He, and many other scientists and mathematicians. The maths point one way only."

Bo grumbled, "But everything in each part!"

The mauve cloud said, "If I show you a colored illustration of the whole visible universe, and you look at it, you see it because it fits on your tiny 2-D retina."

There was a long silence.

The yellow cloud went on, "While intelligent beings in different dimensions might not be able to tell where they really are, Bekenstein said that their brains may be made in such a way as to give them 'an overwhelming commonsense prejudice' that they are seeing one thing or another, just as on your world you feel convinced you see a 3-D world when that could be 'an extraordinary illusion', as he points out.

"He does concede that on your world you generally agree that the universe has matter and radiation spread out pretty evenly and that you call that a 'Friedmann-Robertson-Walker' universe. Your cosmologists mostly agree that your universe is an FRW universe - or hologram - because it has no end and will go on blowing outwards forever.

"However, in 1999, your scientist, Raphael Bousso, at Stanford, came up with a different holographic envelope based on a 2-D surface. That 2-D surface could be folded up into a ball or be spread flat like a piece of paper. His maths stand up, because other holographic models break down with collapsing matter inside a black hole - their boundaries fail. But Brousso's boundary on a 2-D hologram of the world holds fast."

The reddish cloud said, "Bekenstein shows you that your physics of fields has to go, because a field such as the electromagnetic field supposes an infinite freedom for infinite changes. Holography - God's hologram - thwarts freedom, because the boundary won't stretch as fast as the volume inside it. It demands a finite number of freedoms.

"Your scientist Lee Smolin of the Perimeter Institute for Theoretical Physics at Waterlook points out that you have to stop thinking about fields and about spacetime - you have to see that what matters is the exchange of information among all the physical manifestations of the cosmos - of God's creation. God has created a holographic world of information, and of knowing. You wonder whether it is 2-D. Your retinas are 2-D."

There were minutes of silence. Then the blue cloud spoke.

"Edwin Schrödinger told you, 'Mind is a *singulare tantum*, yet all the minds together are but one.' He said that to multiply or divide consciousness is to talk nonsense. We never see more than one consciousness, not even in people with split personalities, he says. Spatio-temporal minds in the plural is false. He wrote, 'I can see no other escape' from this paradox of a single mind embracing all to bring it into a single unit than to abandon the idea of a personality locked inside a human body. The localisation of the conscious mind inside the skull is something we do for convenience only.

"He came close to the great mystery.

"Because on your planet, you humans and your consciousness are part of God's hologram, but God has limited you, chained you in, so that you see but one iota of God's hologram. He has blinded you to the rest."

Fred said aggressively, "How could He do that?"

"Using your lower level, that of your senses. You can see only the stone that you can kick, only the lion that you flush from the thicket. At your middle level, you see more, with language and intelligence... but not much more.

"You see yourselves as a thing in a world of things - as feet that kick stones, as louts who boot the ribs of other louts, as fanged tigers that rip and rend.

"At your higher level, you can enter more and ever more deeply into the hologram of the Primordial One, of the Lord your God, of the Holy Ghost, the Right Hand of the everlasting Godhead."

The four looked stunned.

Bo stuttered," So you're coming back to this idea of our indwelling Spirit. But where is it?"

The blue cloud said, "If you go under, on an operating table, your Spirit can depart your body, still with a strong sense of *you*, but not entirely you.

"It can float to the ceiling and see your body below it; it can float into other rooms and see what is happening there. It can go through a tunnel, to heaven, where the Spirits can compel it to return, even though the YOU in the spirit does not want to return.

"And when you recover, you remember everything. Your Spirit tells your mind what happened, and then your mind knows of your Spirit."

Nicole said, "But only then? Why?"

The blue cloud said, "God has ordained it, because then you tell other people, and the word spreads. Others learn that you have a Spirit. Millions today on earth have had near-death experiences, and told others what happened."

Anne said, "So we know only if we have an out-of-body experience?"

They sat in silence.

The reddish cloud said, "The Spirits are not in space and

time. They can pass through doors, but cannot turn a doorknob. They cannot pick up a spoon."

Bo said, "Some ghosts can."

"A ghost is a force field. Spirits are outside of change and space and time, and so are imperishable, immortal, eternal."

Nicole said, "So nothing ties the brain to the Spirit?"

The beige cloud said, "The neurons in the brain have trillions of synapses, and when we think of glia – that number explodes beyond your comprehension.

"Your neurons are in networks, processing all that comes into the brain, and then that is passed on to your hologram, and into God's hologram. Other human holograms seldom access your input, unless you tell them by voice, or by writing.

"Imagine your brain as a Cray super-computer. It matters not what goes on in the cables of the super-computer. What matters is what a human reads finally on the screen.

"If your brain throws up loyalty, courage, hatred, wonder, these are non-local. If I ask you where is your rose bush, you will tell me it outside your front door. That is its locality.

"Adoration has no locality, no place you can point to. Your brain feeds the hologram. While consciousness seems part and parcel of the brain, it is not. Consciousness lives in your hologram. Your own hologram and your consciousness can act through the brain - telling your legs to walk, your eyes to look.

"Within the hologram, transmission of data is incredibly swift, because every unit is in every part.

"A word springs to your mind. If you had to search for it through brain networks, that could be laborious, although electricity travels through the neurons at 400 kilometers an hour. Little more than a kilometer a second. Slow. But much time is lost with the transmission of neurotransmitters across the synapses.

"Your instantaneous thoughts and associations are in your hologram.

"We are scanning your brains as you sit there. You all fire neurons at random, dissimilar places in your brain for the same words and sentences. We just said 'neurotransmitters' and 'synapses'. Your networks for those words are all over the place on your brains - your brain lighted up in far distant places, one brain compared with the other. We said 'thoughts' and 'hologram'. You each have neuronal networks for those words in far different places on your brains, each scattered in your own way.

"If you depended on your brains to speak, you would each have to open neuronal pathways of your own to connect the word networks. And *keep those pathways open*! And the searches!

"You would each have to open individual, fantastically intricate pathways to your speech centres - and *keep them open*!

"You are not born with safe and sure pathways in your brains. Without a hologram, you would have to try and make them.

"But if each word network broadcasts directly to your

hologram, within your hologram all the word networks are intimately entwined, compacted and touching in the minutest space. Your hologram has a fixed highway to your speech centres.

"Some people's thinking can be mostly visual. That would be slow in the neurons and glia. Michael Faraday was as great in his field as was Newton; he had no mathematics, and his thinking was all visual. He 'saw' the fields around magnets and electrical currents, and he gave your language the words 'lines of force'. He saw these 'lines' filling the whole universe, and he 'saw' light as electromagnetic radiation - a discovery that lay far in the future. He invented the dynamo and electric motor, just visualising them.

"Not one mathematical formula.

"How did he do it?"

They shook their heads.

"His own hologram tapped into the universal hologram of God. He plucked out knowledge that no one could know."

Fred shook his head, in disbelief.

The yellow cloud said, "Do you four see this room?"

They all nodded.

"Did you see our city from the air as your ship came in to dock?"

They nodded again.

"All four of you believe that the city is 'out there', that this room is 'out there', and that you are looking at the walls and ceiling of this room 'out there'."

"That's right," said Fred crisply.

"If you could truly see this room, you would see a colourless electromagnetic haze - and haze is the wrong word.

"Photons strike on your 2-D retina at different wavelengths, and excite your nerves. You build up a neuronal picture inside your skull, and translate the wavelengths into colours. This room exists inside your skull - inside your hologram inside your skull. You project it *outside*, but what you see is *not* outside, but *inside* your head.

"Your picture tells you there is a door three meters away, and a door handle. You take a couple of steps, stretch out your hand, find the handle, and turn it. That confirms that your picture is true, and reinforces your false idea that what is inside your head looks exactly like what is outside.

"If you could truly see outside, you would see something very different to what you project."

They looked worried.

Nicole asked, "What is the interface between the brain and the hologram? For the hologram to order the brain to do something, you would need to exchange energy. If a hologram is made of photons, how can it act on the brain?"

"A hologram can hold every sort of energy. You can have electrons in a hologram.

"The brain unloads into your hologram with photons and electrons and other fields. Your hologram orders your brain to act through a 'mind of God field'."

"What is *that*!" demanded Bo.

"We don't know. The mind of God acts as one field among many fields in the hologram of the whole universe. To know what it is would need a revelation from God. We cannot find that out."

"All these fields," grumbled Anne. "You have light particles *and* waves; that's impossible."

The blue cloud said, "All is vibration, but the observer breaks it into two. In the instant of observing a wave, you can see a particle. It is you, not the physics. You can see lines of force - magnetic lines of force curve down into a topological hole in space without tangling, and vanish. It is how you see them. Another field is the Incomprehensible Mind of the Holy Spirit."

Bo asked, "And when we die, our small hologram goes with a Spirit to heaven - are we to believe that?"

"Your hologram inside your skull belongs to Creation, and cannot enter heaven. When you die, it dissolves, but all the information, all the software of your hologram has already been taken up into the universal hologram, and is in every part of it."

Nicole demanded, "And what good can that information do?"

The beige cloud said, "Do you not read books, study them and learn from other people? Read newspapers, watch television. On billions of planets, beings infinitely more advanced than yourselves - and ourselves - are free to learn."

Bo exclaimed, "Other people on other planets are even more advanced than yourselves?"

"We are a million years old," said the white cloud. "But there are planets with a billion years of civilisation. Our knowledge extended only some seven hundred and fifty light years out - our ships had reached that far, and had had time to send back their information. About a million years ago, we stopped exploring further. Other planets told us of thousands of light years. With new technology, we can travel in days, instead of hundreds of years…"

Anne asked, "And what happens when we die? The Spirit goes up to heaven without us?"

"The Spirit unloads your hologram into its own hologram to take to heaven, to tell all the Spirits there."

Fred said sarcastically, "And what is the Spirit's hologram made of?"

"Godstuff. As your Roman Catholic Pope back on your planet told you, dust goes to dust, but your Spirit is given directly from the hand of God."

Fred muttered, "I don't know a thing about the Pope."

Anne said, "And that dusty hologram within our skulls - what else does it do?"

"It gives you intuition. The Latin word *intueri* means to 'look on', as from an outside point. Inside God's hologram for the whole universe, inside Plato's kingdom of Ideas, the ideas are true ones, and sometimes your tiny hologram can unload some of them into your own skull.

"To 'see' an idea like that, humans can tap their higher level too.

"Your philosopher, William Thompson, has suggested that you humans are 'like flies crawling across the ceiling of the Sistine Chapel.' He warns you that angels are below your threshold of seeing. Does not the physicist Bernard d'Espagnat tell you that you humans are only happy among solid things, like large stones to kick, than among the flowing or invisible?

"Solids for you have a locality. Your car is inside your garage. He tells you that your brains above all deal with information about solids. Primate brains, after millions of years of hominoid life. You survived, he says, with spears and tools made from solids - this in contrast to the flowing, fleeing flesh of animals.

"Humans at their higher level live psychic happenings which shatter space, change and time, and usually others laugh scornfully at them.

"Your famous Carl Jung grew convinced that at this psychic

level all mankind had a common psychic inheritance. It was beyond space and time, and beyond each single mind - all minds were within it. It transcended time because past, present and future 'are blended together in it.'

"From this, he decided that the One Universal Mind and the single personal mind were the same. He concluded that your indwelling Spirit is 'the radiant Godhead itself.'

"He thought consciousness is the impalpable showing forth of the Spiritual."

The orange cloud said, "In your Copenhagen Interpretation of the new physics, Niels Bohr and others said that atoms don't come into your world, and do not leave the universal hologram, until you measure them, or examine them. Of all the possible outcomes of all probabilistic fields, one possibility collapses into an everyday happening. You must combine your personal hologram with the universal one for the new quantum physics to make sense. As your John Wheeler says, the new quantum theory shatters the classical notion of the 'world sitting outside you', with you set well apart. Jacob Bronowski said the same thing about relativity - you can't separate what is happening from the person looking on. Schrödinger said, 'subject and object are only one.'

"Schrödinger turned to the ancient Hindu Vedas and Upanishads to find their answer to what is reality.

"The Mundaka Upanishad says, 'You cannot see him, nor understand him, unborn, never-ending, throughout all is he, without eye or ear, without hands or feet, ever-present, he is the changeless one, the fount of all of us.'

"The Chandaya Upanishad says, 'The universe has as its soul that is you.'

"Schrödinger insisted that you cannot take consciousness away from the world and box it in the brain. Nor can you enclose the self in a body. Your individual mind and self are part of a much greater whole.

"He asks, with so many conscious egos, how do they all see the *same* world? Each human concocts his own world inside his skull; and everyone concocts the *same*. You all think you are looking out at the same place. Why doesn't each of you have his own different world?

"Schrödinger says there is only one answer: that there is only one mind.

"And he is right. God has created but one hologram over the whole universe."

The mauve cloud said, "The hologram in the universe - God created it. Heaven is elsewhere. In your thirteenth century, the Persian mystic, Aziz Nasafi, told you, 'When anything living dies, its spirit goes home to the spiritual realm, and leaves its body in this world. Only the body decays. The spiritual realm is like unto a light behind the bodily world, and when new life comes here, it blazes through it as through a window.

"'Some windows are tall and wide, others small. The light itself is eternally unchanged.'

"But one life, one window. Schrödinger never tired of pointing to this. There is no twofold consciousness – you know only one consciousness. And from God's hand, only one Spirit descends into you, an invisible Spirit unless you suffer temporary clinical death, or near death and God graces you then with knowledge of the Spirit as it leaves your body and then returns.

"Your Spirit is seamless. Your Sir Charles Sherrington told you that he found energy and matter as 'grainy', but not consciousness.

"How can you know that God is from everlasting to everlasting? Because in your modern physics past, present and future no longer exist. Not one experiment has shown that time runs like an ever-flowing river. There is no outside world where time could measure change. Schrödinger tried to tell you - consciousness is always *now*. You cannot be conscious in the *before* or in the *future*. You are only conscious *now* - you might remember yesterday or worry about tomorrow. He said that Mind could never be destroyed because it was outside time, in the *now*.

"Time comes from change - you measure the change with clocks, and call your measurement *time*.

"He says you live in a present eternal life. When time stops, eternity steps in. The now is eternally and forever now, he tells you. The only thing that never ends is the present."

131

The orange cloud said, "But we can never understand the utter intricacy of God's laws within the universal hologram. Your mythical Kurt Gödel, one of your planet's greatest mathematicians, told you in your year of 1931 that a rich logical system can never become complete, and secondly, you can never be sure it will be consistent.

"Completeness and perfection lie in heaven; in the universes and dimensions, the Holy Ghost has created a lesser order of being which may appear real, but can never be. So your minds think about yourselves - but you have only your minds to think with. And God smiles. Gödel's Incompleteness Theorem says that you can never draw a full and consistent portrait of nature. God has ordained it so, and Gödel shows that it cannot be done. His Theorem shows that if God's laws *are* consistent, they will be incomprehensible to us.

"In 1977, the mathematician Rudy Rucker talked to Gödel on the phone, and asked Gödel did he believe in a single Mind behind the multiplicity of surface forms.

"Gödel said, 'yes', and that the Mind is separate from all its properties. He said to get rid of the notion of time passing, and to seek the mystic *now*. He said you think of time as passing because you think of change in different realities.

"He said, there is only one reality, and we live seeing different 'givens'. Images seen by our small hologram in the universal hologram, realities given there by God."

Fred shook his head. "Images. Realities. *Given*."

The reddish cloud said, "Every sort of field fills the hologram, and waves, vibrations in the fields give us particles. Lumps in a custard. Are you never surprised that light *always* travels at the speed of light? It doesn't start off slower, and accelerate up. That all the gold atoms have exactly the same mass? Every electron has the same mass, charge and spin? Each particle gets exactly the energy it needs and never goes for lack? When you see refrigerators coming off a factory line, and they are exactly the same, don't you think you see design there? In Europe, all euro coins have the same value - in the United States, all one-cent pieces are the same. Do you think that just happened - that a typhoon came along and made them?

"In the hologram of the Universal God, every living consciousness, every corporeal thing has its place. The hologram is unbroken, its particles and forms repeated everywhere. Your classical science taught a world of independent bits, on their own, and you still think like that.

"Do you not all see the same world inside your heads? Particles of different wavelengths strike your 2-D retinas. You know not which particles came from a short distance, and which from a far distance. But everyone converts the wavelengths into the same colors - unless someone suffers brain damage, which changes and falsifies those wavelengths on their way.

"You convert those identical particles into near objects and far objects, and when you measure the distances and sizes, all the measurements are the same.

"All your holograms are tapping into the same universal hologram. You transcribe the incoming particles into a whole physical world inside your skulls, and you have but one picture of the world in six billion brains on your planet. A single God consciousness has made a single picture, a Single, Universal Mind. With oceans of sensory data that your billions of brains process each second, there is no chaos, no total collapse of converse, of transmittal between one human and another when they speak the same language.

"Yet, each human's brain is disparate, unlike its fellows."

Fred said, "We make the same picture because there's only one world out there to make the picture from."

The eight sat in silence.

The mauve cloud said, "There is no world out there, as you understand it. There are only force fields and particles outside of your skull."

The white cloud said, "Well, let us grant that we speak in allegories, in metaphors. Reality is the one supreme, self-determined ground of all variety that we see, not singled out from anything else. We are part of it, in an incomprehensible way, but not just a 'part' singled out from something else, but at one level, we *are* the One Mind, as Schrödinger says. Each human is part of God, of the Universal One, but set about by severe boundaries - you see but a minute part of it because of the lower level of your brains, because of your five senses."

Anne muttered, "But our minds depend on the chemistry of the body and the brains!"

"Indeed," said the yellow cloud. "Yet another limiting boundary to lock you in with. One day, your biologists will learn from your physicists. Physics on your world moves towards fields while your biologists and Darwinists are lost in some sort of nineteenth century classical physics - in some sort of mechanical world, where chemistry and electricity would abolish mind.

"Your biologists and Darwinists are retreating to a rock-solid materialism when physics has found that the materialistic phenomena are an illusion, a penumbra... that mind participates in matter and change, even at the level of particles.

"Did not Niels Bohr tell you that he could not find anything in physics and chemistry that had an even remote influence on consciousness.

"And he was right. Consciousness can influence chemistry and physics, but not the other way around. Well, you can administer poisons, and shut off the brain. Then you close off the hologram and consciousness, and possibly free the Spirit to leave the body, perhaps to return a little later.

"Are you living in the 1750s? Then the famed Julien de La Mettrie laid down that 'man is a machine'."

Bo said, "You can't deny that when you get to a certain complexity, the 'mind' appears, and not before."

The green cloud said, "Your great philosopher of science, Karl

Popper, said that was a meaningless thing to say. He said that how little was said with 'that mind was emergent from the brain.' The words explained nothing - all they did was put a big question mark at a certain point on the road of humanity's progress.

"'Emergent'! Your indwelling Spirit is *not* of time and space and can do nothing, not even lift up a spoon, in the created world. How can non-material mind act on material matter - on, say, nerves leading to arms and legs? Your hologram can act because it - and God's hologram - *are* within space and time.

"In classical physics, for one entity to influence another, you need an exchange of energy. You need an exchange of energy to push someone into a swimming pool.

"Your non-material hologram is wholly free of the brain but it can influence it without energy exchange between them. Modern physics has seen this again and again - but your biology still says it is impossible.

"And where energy *is* needed, the brain can supply it.

"Imagine the lonely Scottish moors, and a small loch about fifty meters across; the never-ending Scots winds send criss-crossing ripples across the peat darkened waters. So are mind and 'matter' - crossing vibrations. The fields which have sway over consciousness and those that direct the continuum of matter are fields within fields within fields."

Anne said, "Let's get our feet back on solid ground... back up a bit there. What bothers me is that there's nothing practically outside me - that *can't* be right. I can see this room, damn it."

The green cloud said, "You don't have to believe us. Back on earth, your Heinz Von Foerster, a cyberneticist, has told you that your retinas are practically 'blind'. They don't see anything, but respond to particles. He asks why are people surprised.

"He says that 'out there' there is no noise, no voices, no shouts, no sound of traffic, no music - total silence. Only changes in the air pressure. There is no colour, no green trees and red roses, only electromagnetic waves. He says that 'out there' there's no heat or cold, only molecules moving with more or less kinetic energy. Out there is no pain..."

"Then what is *real*?" demanded Anne.

"God is real. Nothing else. Your indwelling Spirit is real, given to you from the very hand of the Godhead."

Anne gnawed her lip. After a couple of minutes, she said, "I asked you about this quantum business, and you still haven't answered me."

The reddish cloud said, "With the discovery of X-rays humans could search for atoms at last. But you found radioactivity, which proved there was something even smaller than atoms.

"While Rutherford found that radioactive substances emitted alpha particles, Max von Laue used X-rays to find the layout of atoms in crystals.

"Then Rutherford bombarded atoms with high-speed alpha-particles and got a serious shock. Since the fifth century BC, mankind had believed atoms were solid building blocks - now

Rutherford found they were immense, vast empty space, with incredibly distant electrons orbiting around them.

"He found that if you blow an atom up to the size of a small, round playing field, the protons and neutrons would be grains of salt in the middle with the electron orbiting around the edge. Rutherford found that so-called 'matter' is mostly empty regions of space. The electrons go at 600 miles a second – the 'grains of salt' circle each other at 44,000 miles a second.

"Then humans would find that the electromagnetic force held the electron in its orbit, and the strong force held the grains of salt together - the protons and neutrons. It would take an atom bomb to break the strong force, and a hydrogen bomb to create the strong force to join them.

"Along came the quantum physicists like Planck and Heisenberg and others, and soon a myriad of sub-atomic particles came to light. They did not act like physical objects.

"These sub-atomic particles can appear as a particle or as a wave. Particles are crammed into a small bit of space, the waves spread way, way out. Your language has nothing to cope with this, and Heisenberg wrote that he asked himself the question over and again, 'Could nature be so absurd?'

"The paradox of particle and wave was incomprehensible. Nature wasn't just weird, but more eldritch than anyone could ever hope to imagine. Words weren't enough. As the ancient Chinese Tao said, 'You use fishing baskets to catch fish, but when you land the fish, men forget the baskets... You use words to disclose ideas; when men understand, they forget the words.'

"Waves are circles of probability – somewhere, on them, is the particle.

"Humans were to be further dumbfounded. Near the end of the nineteenth century, Max Planck found that heat does not radiate continuously but in separate packets of energy. Einstein called the packet *quanta*, and thence you get the name *quantum*. Light, too, propagates as particles called photons somewhere on their probability waves. But it propagates in quanta, and always travels at the speed of light.

"Electrons too. Sometimes they look like particles, but they can spread widely over space. They don't *exist*, but tend to exist. Neither as particles nor as a wave packet can we say exactly where they are, nail down their locality.

"Mankind was looking at ideas in God's hologram.

"Next Einstein found that the nothingness of space curves around heavenly bodies. Imagine a steel ball lying on a sheet of rubber - the rubber sinks. Curvature controls gravity and gravity curves space.

"Empty curved space gives life to force fields of electromagnetism, charge, atoms ... all of God's geometry. Behind the force fields are strings, quarks, protons... all vibrations in curved space. The vibrations cause dense energy 'lumps' in the fields, lumps that we see as particles; the vibrations cause waves.

"The paradox of particles and waves is simply one of geometry, of undulations 'intersecting' as it were. Gentle curves give gravity; rippled fields, electromagnetism. High, lumpy curvature gives concentrations of mass-energy and charged particles.

"What the physicists decided finally was that every point in space is directly close to every other point. Then they suggested the hologram, where points not touching in space are yet in bosom contact.

"In the   slit experiment, a beam of particles travels at the same speed. When the particles hit the slit and go through, some will change direction, and will hit a sensitive detection screen over a wider range than the slit.

"Schrödinger's Equation tells us that 10 percent of particles will hit one place, and the other 90 percent will hit another area. If you take one hundred particles, and send them through the slit one by one, you cannot predict where they will go until 10 of them have hit one place. Then you can be sure the rest will go to the other screen.

"Einstein would not accept quantum theory. He said that God does not play dice in the universe; but the old classical universe of cause and effect was dead.

"How do the particles *know* that the quota of ten percent has been filled, and the rest must go to the second area? What cosy, secret knowledge do they share, although they are separated, and go through the slit one by one? How could they transmit the information? They behave as a single entity, not as separate particles sending signals."

Bo said, "What's this about playing dice?"

The blue cloud said, "Your classical physics saw the universe as a clock. Laws were unbreakable, guaranteed what would happen next.

"Before the quantum scientists, your William Gibbs had already said that the universe was unpredictable, except within statistical probabilities.

"The Earth circles the sun almost in exactly the same way each time. When you press a light switch, you are almost sure it will work. You can be almost certain that when you turn on the ignition of your car, the engine will fire.

"But occasionally, the switch fails, the engine doesn't start up.

"The chances of getting scratches on the bodywork of your car each day are much higher. So are the chances of it raining. To fly in a jet is safer than in a propeller plane; it is also safer than in a train; and a train is safer than a car; a car is safer than a motorbike; and a motorbike is safer than a horse.

"Your insurance companies can tell you.

"The universe - your own life - is a hierarchy of probabilities. Nothing's certain except the death of your body.

"The probability of lightning killing you is low, but the chance of catching a cold in the next twelve months is high.

"Physicists no longer say what always happens, but what happens more often, or less often.

"In classical physics, human scientists believed in cause and effect because of the extremely high probabilities in, say, astrophysics. They confused extremely high probabilities with permanency. Now you have to work out probabilities not only in this universe, but in parallel universes, in the shuffling of many probabilistic universes.

"Today, the fate of individual particles has no meaning - your scientists look to the hologram for general behaviour. Particles can branch out into infinite universes of possibility - when a mind decides, there is a collapse into one universe, which is ours. The ghost of consciousness has entered the laws of physics.

"You live in a colossal number of parallel universes, with infinite possible outcomes - each choice you make collapses reality into one universe, one outcome. In the quantum world, chance rules supreme. Every quantum change on every star splits the universe into a countless host of collapsed realities, whose outcome was pure chance before the collapse decided what would finally happen.

"This does not happen with biological systems. Here we see the Hand of God. Outside fields determine what happens at every instant, and the cells exchange magnetic and electrodynamic signals among themselves.

"While physicists struggled to accept a universe of chance, biologists have tried to thrust Darwinism down humanity's throat. Cells all respond to where they are in the whole, and the field tells them where to settle and in what direction to point. A cell divides into two, and, like a hologram, each half has complete information about the original whole. Biology works in a directed hologram, and lacks the random freedom of the wind, of the rain, of astronomical dust clouds, burning and exploding stars, colliding galaxies...

"Any unity in the universe is the sameness of its force fields. But all parts are connected in the Universe, as they are in the human body. Germs in a hand can affect your whole body and your whole life.

"While chance rules the universe, instruments can measure its force fields.

"You cannot isolate one part of the universe - every part is an intimate part of the whole. Subsystems can be small, or they can reach from one side of the universe to the other - but you cannot separate out any sub-system. It is a dynamic hologram where every part of the net fires the whole net at once.

"The *Avatamsaka Sutra* of ancient Hindu scriptures tells you of Indra's net. In Indra's heaven, pearls are woven into a web, so that when you look at one you see all the others shining in it."

Fred said, "But how do our thoughts get into this, er, hologram?"

The yellow cloud said, "The countless networks of neurons,

with electricity racing at 400 kilometers an hour process all the incoming particles. They build electromagnetic fields, force fields, mind fields, which pass into the hologram, by photons, electrons and other particles. Inside the hologram, every unit is cross-referenced with every thought.

"You think of *intimate*, and, upon the instant, words like *lover, friend, close, dear, deep, home...* they flash into your consciousness without effort, much faster than neural networks could recover and present them. Words like *smile, mountain* and *pubic hair* produce other words and images in a twinkling, in the smallest conceivable lapse of time.

"Your consciousness is a small continuum in an unimaginably vast continuum of vibrating fields, and that is why some humans can influence matter. When you pass electrons through a slit, some scientists find they can tell each electron where to go. Other people predicted the sinking of the Titanic, and one man published a book exactly describing what happened twenty years earlier. Hundreds of years ago, a Roman Catholic priest levitated over and again, in front of the Pope and other princes - the church made him a saint. Men can walk across beds of coals heated to hundreds of degrees.

"Your field is a field within fields within fields within the Mind of God."

Nicole complained, "Religion doesn't teach these things."

Fred asked cunningly, "What do you think religion should do on earth?"

The white mind mist said, "We do not interfere with what happens on earth."

"And on an imaginary planet, what would you expect from religion?" demanded Fred.

The white cloud said, "On an imaginary planet, with reading and writing, and with planetwide communications, with violence still... Still. Let us come back to your planet. For more than a thousand years, humans mingled the 'facts' of science and religion. Science and religion both accepted as fact that an Almighty Being created the world. But, between Thomas Aquinas, Rene Descartes, and others, the two schools split their ways, in a mode we don't see on other planets in the Confederation.

"Back on your earth, religion inherited God, the soul, after-life and ethics. Science held fast to space and matter and velocity, to measurement.

"When we come up to your twentieth century, science encroached into evolution and attacked religion's God, soul and after-life. Religion lost badly.

"Religion beat a retreat and shifted ground – now religion did not deal so much in facts. Your Paul Tillich said that science tells you about nature, religion about the meaning of life.

"Today, many of your Christian thinkers stand on that unsteady ground of *meaning*, and will usually take any detour, serious detours, not to run into scientists over *facts*.

"What has that brought you to? Today, on your planet, most

people in the advanced west suppose that the Great Hologram is limited to rough, dross matter, to living creatures and to daily states of consciousness.

"Science has staked out this ground through physics and biology, and then announced to the world at large that anything beyond all this was a matter for faith, if not the occult.

"Spiritual mystics undergo rigid disciplines over years, and enter into the higher level of their consciousness to go into the hologram, to approach God Himself, beyond the hologram.

"But on your planet, hundreds of millions don't listen. They stick to their five senses, their lower level of perception.

"The great religions have told what their mystics have found - told you over thousands of years. This has profoundly transformed your minds without your knowing. But conservative religious believers have circled their wagons and call much of that spiritual activity recusant and a hazard."

"Where will religion go?" asked Anne.

The white mind mist said, "We do not interfere."

The yellow cloud repeated, "On an imaginary planet, with reading and writing, with planetwide communications, with violence still…"

The cloud was silent for a minute, then said, "Traditional religion usually shows morality, and proper social living together. As do the Ten Commandants and the Golden Rule on your own planet. Traditional religion offers on countless planets for the congregation, and on your planet, forgiveness of your sins. What are these 'sins'?

"On an imaginary planet, religion could take congregations to a higher understanding, that God created all things, but things and God are not outside you as an ignorant flock might falsely imagine. On your planet, the Roman Catholic Teilhard de Chardin teaches, 'Matter is transparent.'

"Ignorant religious flocks on an imaginary planet I would think need to learn that one part of the Everlasting God within the cosmos is ever formless and illimitable, indefinable; but His other aspect is multiple, visible, because He has created all things."

The orange cloud said, "Possibly, on an imaginary planet, the churches could teach about consciousness, which from outside looks like energy fields in the hologram; but from within it is awareness illuminated by the eternal indwelling Spirit.

"A sacred task it would be, to transmute consciousness, as we have done, and as have so many planets."

The blue cloud said, "Possibly, on an ideal planet, priests and pastors would ask themselves – 'If I am taken to judgement over my flock, on what shall I be judged? Have I illuminated, enlightened them?' On many planets we see this."

The beige cloud said, "On an imaginary planet, the religious could remember that helping and uplifting others makes love grow. And for those who follow paths of love, waiting on others, laboring for them, makes love flower.

"Also, the flocks would fret over the needy, over social wrongs and cruelty, in compassion and care, would fight violence and war."

Fred snapped, "And what about a just war?"

The white cloud said, "Ah! What is a just war? A just war is one where they will invade you, and subject you to exploitation, torture and death — then you must fight with the sorrowing strength of God."

The mauve cloud said, "Religions on such a planet could teach that atheism is but a passing step on a long road.

"They should carry the knowledge of immortality and life after death to all the peoples. Perhaps they would come to terms with the paranormal - not sham chimera - but that which has no divide from what we imagine to be normal, something their Gospels could honor."

The yellow cloud said, "Such religions could teach the ordinary people the difference between daily consciousness and states of noumenal consciousness.

"They could teach what their scientists might well have already found - that they live among appearances, when in fact they live among God's hyperspaces, and that mathematics is one of God's first tools in His creation."

The orange cloud said, "On an imaginary planet? I would urge their religions to teach that angels abide among them, in a countless host, that those who see angels do not hallucinate."

Bo scoffed, "Angels!"

The white cloud said, "What will you four do when you go back? Can you speak of this and save your professional careers?"

The four looked frightened.

"Archangels and angels from today will care for you and your futures."

They stared at the white mind-mist, stunned.

After a long silence, the reddish cloud said, "For the religious on a densely populated planet cut off for far too long from spirituality - a planet we would have to seek far and wide to find anything as bad - for those religious I would think they should teach God."

After a long silence, Fred said patiently, "You talk about God. We have never seen him. We have no proof - hard proof - that there is a God."

Anne asked, "Who are the aliens on earth, or flying around our planet?"

The beige cloud said, "Some are interstellar, some inter-dimensional. Some are tangible – bodily - others more 'cloudy', more energy than matter."

The white cloud said to Fred, "You talk of proof of God. What proof have you ever seen in your life? Your lower level of perception serves to flush a lion out of a thicket, build cars or jet planes. You kill the lion, drive the car or fly the plane, and say, see!

It works. Your polluted planet attests to that. Do you want to go back to a tribal village and hunt with a spear for the satisfaction of knowing you have a total knowledge and command of reality?

"You humans have a lower level of perception, your senses. What are you perceiving? You have not the least idea of the world outside your skull.

"You have only the technicolor hologram inside your head.

"At your middle level, you have mind.

"If you finish the long discipline of studying to be a fossil hunter, people will believe what you tell them, although they have no personal, direct knowledge themselves, inside their skulls, at their middle level.

"At mankind's higher level, you have meditation, transcendency, enlightenment, revelation, Divine Reality outside of space and time. Mystics undergo a long, rigid discipline, but in the western countries, you don't heed them.

"In the East, on your planet, they do.

"What is proof? At your lower level, it tells you that if you see, hear or feel this, do that.

"At your middle level, it tells you, if you *know* this, do that.

"What bedevils you humans, hypnotizes and confounds you, is that at your lower and middle levels you have an immediate grasping of what is given, of the data supplied.

"You go by *givens*, and believe them to be absolute!

"But for the mass of humanity, the givens are instantaneously realised, in a flash are captured, at the sensory and mental levels only.

"Those levels *give* you *sensibilia* and *intelligibilia* only. Your higher level of perception, the spiritual, deals with *transcendelia*, which is as remote to your understanding as travelling one thousand light years in three days."

Nicole said, "If we are here?"

The beige cloud said, "You can take photos. There will be so little difference in the sky as not to matter."

Anne asked, "This is your planet?"

The white cloud said, "We come from three hundred light years away."

"How did you get here!" exclaimed Anne.

The beige cloud said, "We got here before we left. And when we send you back, you will arrive at your house in the Rocky Mountains before you left. At the moon, a disk will let you off at four o'clock in the morning on the day you left. Darkness will hide the disk."

Bo exploded, "And we go into the house and see ourselves sleeping!"

The beige cloud said, "Those bodies will fade, will collapse into another dimension to live different lives. We are talking about very advanced physics."

151

After a silence, the white mind-mist said, "Your lower level, your sensory level, is empirical, and there you humans go off the rails. Empirical data. It is given to you on the moment, instant perception, and that dazzles you.

"At the middle level, that data can be images, a letter, a word, a sentence, a fleeting notion or a full idea, an equation, a geometrical abstraction, memory of a fossil bone - but again, you have a capture in a twinkling.

"You may think of tomorrow's appointment, your return to the Rocky Mountains - you directly seize these thoughts in a fraction of a second.

"And you are convinced it is real 'activity'. That if you order those thoughts with logic, you will have a proof in your lap.

"Your mother tongue is the same. You speak and understand sentences by unthinking reflex. As everyone does the same, you have found another 'truth'.

"Where do you go wrong? You are forever mixing up your levels. Darwin took fossils which he saw and handled at his lower level, then laid down the law verbally at the middle level, and you accept his words as gospel. The fossils do not prove what Darwin says.

"You demand empirical, lower level proof of the trans-universe of your higher level. You judge the higher by the lower, and especially by the middle level.

"What is your middle level? It is good for naming craters on the far side of the moon, for telling a tribesman to turn around and look at a thicket where there *might* be a tiger - for understanding Shakespeare or Mesopotamian cuniform, for grasping monetarism or economic geography.

"This is a level for mapping, for comparing, for conjecture, but its grasp of theories denotes no grasp of the divine God.

"Levels are *different*! At your lower level, that of *sensibilia*, you can measure and weigh. You can measure the length, width, height and weight of a metal component of a car engine.

"How much does wisdom weigh? How do you measure love, idealism and bliss? *Intelligibilia* has no extension to measure.

"What your lower and middle levels bestow upon your consciousness, vouchsafe it for it to take in a flash - what it furnishes was in very large part to keep a primate alive one million, several million years ago, and is not what consciousness on other planets necessarily find, are vouchsafed.

"With what desperate trust do you clasp it. Does not what it furnishes show you how to build machines that work well and pollute your planet? What could be more trustworthy?

"At the level of *transcendelia*, a given may be a sole spiritual illumination, an immediately grasped *gnosis*.

"Ah! 'Grasping' - well and good! But grasping in *transcendelia*... You don't want to accept that.

"The rub is in the grasping, the apprehension, the capture, the seizure of data served up to you.

"At the lower level, it means for you empirical sensory data - something you can grab, we might venture to say.

"At the middle level, it can cover an almost limitless field of awareness, of knowing. Your ideas, your *mentalese* - that unceasing, turbulent stream of consciousness - they thrust themselves into your mind's eye, into your consciousness, and you receive them as absolutely real. You *receive* them, you live them. What your mind's eye grasps, you accept. That's your *real* you.

"It is not.

"Another eye, your spiritual eye, not your mind's eye, can receive, undergo, can realise the spiritual as divine, a direct meeting, a givenness from God.

"At your lower level, are you supplied with mathematics? Some humans master mathematics at their middle level, and the rest of you accept what has been bestowed on their consciousness when they report it - accept without understanding one single line of mathematical formulae.

"Empiricism on the planet earth is on solid ground - your senses must be able to measure it, hold it, see it...

"But woe! if you demand empiricism at your middle level, insist you must encounter your mathematics, your language, through *sensations!* You can't. This is a gross mixing of levels, and humanity has shown its artistry in mixing. Artists in error!

"The truth is that you *do not* know what is outside of your head. Your image of this room is a *given*, not a direct grasping, and you all lust after sensory proof. You think you have sensory knowledge of this room - but you do not. It is a raging haze of colorless particles.

"Your science has made some progress. Now Thomas Kuhn tells you to investigate through *paradigms*, by conjecture, by unproved theory, and round up all the data on your search that you can.

"This means that you can find yourself raking in data that is non-sensual, not from the senses, but from your middle intelligible level - because it fits precisely, on all sides, and without it, you can't finish.

"Sir Karl Popper tells you that you must try to falsify what you are doing. You must be able to try and disprove it, and see you cannot disprove it.

"What happens at the middle level is disclosure - mathematical, linguistic, geometrical... whatever. At this middle level, to know language is the same as practising meditation at the higher level; contemplation at the higher level is as logic for your middle level.

"The seeker at the higher level, the mystic, knows himself not just as one individual, bounded about by his body - as thus he knows himself at the middle and lower level - but as standing before the Ultimate Absolute, the All, the everlasting, illimitable boundlessness of the Infinite God.

"This transcendental Path is one which many have trod, and all have reported the same. As an experiment, it is repeatable, verifiable, an experiment repeated so often over thousands of years as to constitute proof of God in creation, of the Holy Ghost, of the Holy Spirit, of the Right Hand of the Godhead in the cosmos.

"This is your higher *level*. On your planet, your Plotonius told you, 'How can we know the Infinite One? My answer is, not by reason'. Then Pascal added to that. 'The heart has its reasons, which reason cannot know.'

"Reason is of your middle level. And on your middle level, funnily, you are actually on sounder ground with your interior accepting of words, ideas, matter, abstractions, logic than on your lower level. At the middle, you have a much stronger given.

"But it is blind, empty and silent before the transcendent."

Bo said stubbornly, "What we still have is somebody declaring info we can't check."

The white cloud said, "You can't check how we got you here in three days - you can't check our tachyonic jets, tachyonic fields."

Bo muttered, "That's if we are ten million light-years away."

The white mind-mist said, "We will let you take a suitcase full of photos back with you."

Anne cried, "If we show those, they'll lock us up as lunatics!"

The beige cloud said, "What a shambles! Contradictions! You humans are invincibly ignorant. What a planet - violent killers, polluters! What mental processes!"

Fred said sourly, "A slum planet."

The mauve cloud said, "You have said it. They are your words, not ours."

Nicole said, "Please go on about God."

After a long pause, the white cloud went on. "Gnosis is direct knowledge of the spirit, of the spiritual.

"The spiritual discernment, the spiritual encounter, is beyond the fallible middle level, with its middle knowledge, language, theory and conjecture; it is the grasping of transcendental spirituality, instantly, through the indwelling Spirit, leading one to God.

"They are spiritual states of consciousness in which space, time, the ego and all ideas vanish as the Spirit perceives and joins the absolute God, joins with the pure, radiant Being itself.

"Space-time expands till it disappears in the encompassing All, in the Eternal Present, the *nunc stans*, the Timeless immortal Present which is beyond time.

"The Spirit rises above the dross hard matter, passing through consciousness and abstraction, and through an ever-growing transparency of space and time - rises into the measureless, immutable, unchanging, limitless reality of God... and the now nameless, formless consciousness unites with the Eternal Light blazing with Love, the Divine Formless Presence, the unending Radiance and Bliss, the Infinite Refulgence and Glory that is God."

PART THREE

The mauve cloud said, "It is time for you to return."

The white cloud said, "Do you wish us to wipe all memory of this from your minds?"

After several minutes, the four shook their heads. Leather pouches appeared in front of them.

The beige cloud said, "Those pouches hold large, flawless diamonds of great price. You will never need to fear for your university tenures.

"Buy combination safes, and put the diamonds inside. No one will ever break into those safes. When you spend those diamonds, more will appear, while you live. If peer reviews condemn you, and you cannot get published, you can launch your own journal."

After a long silence, Bo said, "We left our wheels parked off to one side of a mountain road."

"Aliens have driven your wheels back to the house."

Anne said, "I would like to keep in touch."

"Aliens will keep in touch."

Nicole said, "Could we sometimes take our holidays on board a ship, or on the moon?"

The white cloud said, "Granted."

The disk went down to thirty feet above the road outside their house.

A ramp tongued out, and they walked down it unsteadily. It was four o'clock in the morning, and very dark.

They stood and watched the ramp retract; the disk rose swiftly, humming.

Inside the house, they sat at the dining-room table, and Nicole emptied her diamonds on to the wooden table top.

Everyone stared at them.

Fred said, "I suggest coffee, and maybe something to eat. The store down the road opens at six o'clock, so we gotta get there on time."

Anne exclaimed, "The store!"

Fred said, "To buy a newspaper."

Anne shook her head. "A newspaper!"

Fred said, "To see if the date's the twenty-second."

After a moment, Bo said, "It will be. But let's go anyway and make sure."

The End